When We Had Feathers

Tales from the Angels' Share
Volume 6

Marella Sands

Word Posse

Dedication

To Pastor Brian, my cohort in commentary for my YouTube playlist "Infernal Intercourse," and all-around great person.

The Angels' Share Books

Volume 1: Through a Keyhole, Darkly
Volume 2: What the Thunder Said
Volume 3: The Chair She Sat In
Volume 4: With Sleepless Eye
Volume 5: Past the Isle of Dogs
Volume 6: When We Had Feathers
Volume 7: Feeding the Bird of Tondal (coming in 2021)

Other Word Posse Books by Marella Sands

Pandora's Mirror
Fortune's Daughter
Restless Bones

Ring of Fire Press Books by Marella Sands

Perdition
Purgatory
Perfection
Paradise (coming in 2021)
Promised Land (coming in 2022)

Catch up with the author on various platforms:
Facebook: facebook.com/MarellaSands
YouTube: Search *Marella Sands* once there!

This book has been typeset in Fanwood. Cover design by Word Posse.

ISBN-13: 978-1-944089-80-1

Praise for *Restless Bones*

"Marella Sands has a keen eye for detail, and an ability to take innocent research and bits of trivia, and turn them into stories that will disturb, frighten, charm, and make you think." Laurell K. Hamilton

"I think Marella Sands may have made a horror short-story fan out of me!" Kaylee Stevens

"Haunting and engrossing, this compilation of tales of spine-tingling horror will have you on the edge of your seat." Brenda Maxwell

"The stories are a great length to read in one sitting—if you can take it! I had goose bumps throughout." Nicole Hastings

"A must read for fans of horror and dark fantasy." Stacy Decker

"I was pleasantly surprised by the top-notch professionalism in this book, from the strength of the narration to the engaging storylines—a real challenge considering the shorter length of these stories. Kudos to Ms. Sands; she will be on my list of authors to watch." Max Gilbert

Praise for *Pandora's Mirror*

"This was a brilliant novel and very well-crafted. I was most impressed with the amazing writing—literary, beautiful, almost poetic prose that made the story even creepier to read." Essie Harmon

"The writing is simply lovely, with literary prose that has powerful, evocative word choices that truly bring this terrifying story to life. A fast read with shocking twists, and a satisfying ending." Nicole Hastings

"Warning—when starting Pandora's Mirror, make sure you don't have anywhere you need to be or anything you need to do because you won't want to stop reading until you've finished it all!" Stacy Decker

1

"How stupid can you be?" shouted my boss, Ware, at myself and my boyfriend Castro.

Castro looked cowed, but I wasn't. I didn't care if Ware were angry. This was his fault. Everything was his fault. Anger rose up my throat.

"Well, frankly, I don't know," I spat out. "Because you haven't said. Maybe, if you would like me to make good choices, you should provide good information first."

Ware opened his mouth, and then closed it again. His red face faded slightly and his breathing slowed. The whiskey bottles behind him rattled slightly where they stood on the glass shelves behind the bar. Weird. But then, that's what you got for working for a supernatural creature.

"I haven't wanted to burden you with everything all at once," he said, still loudly, and only somewhat more reasonably. "There's so much."

"Because you're immortal and this war you all had with each other spanned galaxies, and destroyed them," I said.

Castro blanched at that. Surely, I'd mentioned the war involving the destruction of stars and galaxies my boss had been involved in. The one where he'd been the general in one camp, and his best friend had led the other.

Brother against brother. With creatures that didn't have brothers, as far as I knew. But they did have friends. Lovers.

Love triangles, even. It should have been boring, like any stupid romcom where the girl can't choose between the nice guy and the bad boy. Except, with these guys, there was that *galaxy-destroying* aspect to it. And the part where that war was heating up again.

The war my boss believed I'd be playing a major part in.

Like any human could do much against an entire race that could do things like snuff out stars.

Castro shook his head. "Look, I have no idea what's going on here, but it's clear Teryl has to have a higher level of knowledge, whether you like it or not, whether it's a good idea or not."

"No one asked you," barked my boss.

"Hey," I said. "You speak to him like that again, and I'm out of here."

Ware actually did a double-take, which was something I'd only read about. People don't actually *do* that, right? Except Ware acted as if he'd been struck and his eyes got wide.

The brand on my right palm, the one that spelled out Ware's name in some archaic script that I doubted had even been developed on this planet, suddenly struck me with a burning pain. I clenched my hand into a fist and managed not to yelp.

I couldn't help but clamp my mouth shut and grimace, though. Ware noticed. The struggle to control his emotions raged across his face a few moments before he managed to take a deep breath.

My heart slowed slightly. I might not take any guff off my boss, but that didn't make him any less scary.

"Fine," he said. "Describe what was taken. I know what it should be, but maybe I'm wrong."

"It was a red feather," I said. "A small one, soft, almost like down. It protected me from the fire at Cahokia. But it doesn't look anything like what, um, *you* looked like before."

"Before?" asked Castro. His dark eyes were puzzled.

"Before Earth?" I asked. "Before the war? I don't really know. It was just that, for a little while, I saw Oya the way she appeared in the past. All angles and crystal and metal." Those words bothered me; what I had seen hadn't really fit into what I thought of as *crystalline* or *metallic*, but those were the best words I had. "No softness, no fluffy wings. Nothing that you'd recognize from an Earth-based myth or legend."

I looked at Ware expectantly.

"That was, indeed, one of our forms," he said. "Originally, we didn't have physical form. We just existed. But we learned to manipulate matter to the point where we could create bodies. We sailed the void on wings constructed out of materials you have no words for. You couldn't even imagine the life we led back then."

Of that, I had no doubt.

"And now you run a bar in St. Louis?" asked Castro. "Isn't that a bit of a come-down?"

"Depends on what you mean by that," said Ware. He glanced around the dimly-lit interior of the Angels' Share bar, which he owned, and which was, technically, still my place of employment. I hadn't actually had a regular shift in a while. Not since Ware had decided to pay me just to stick around and run errands for him. You know, because I was important to the cause or whatever. "No, we don't travel between the stars anymore. But that doesn't mean life on Earth doesn't have its attractions and benefits."

I tried to imagine living life on Earth as an ordinary person after having spent millions, if not billions, of years going anywhere in the universe I wanted, seeing creation and destruction everywhere as stars were born, lived, and died around me. And then settling for a human-looking body and a life among barely sentient apes with a penchant for pollution, cruelty, and ennui.

Many people managed to live boring colorless lives of only a few decades. How could one live on Earth and not eventually get bored like that? It would take longer, I would suppose, than decades, but eventually, how boring would life on Earth be?

"So, back to the feather," I said, dismissing the fantastical vision of sailing the universe on wings. I bit back a yawn. Jet lag sucked. I'd just gotten in to town from London a little over a day ago and wasn't yet recovered from the flight, not to mention all the walking and running and fighting the entire trip had involved. "It belongs to one of you?"

"You know whose it is," he said. "Who hasn't been around lately?"

I'd hardly been at the bar enough lately to know who was in and out as per usual. But clearly, Ware thought I should know who hadn't been in, which meant I should consider the short list of the people who came often.

People with red flecks in their hair and irises, perhaps? The same red as the feather?

"Fish," I said.

Ware nodded.

Castro visibly relaxed. "Oh, Fish? I thought you meant one of those, like those, who, uh..."

"Tried to kill you?" I asked.

"Yeah. Them."

"Marveaux and Garnett wouldn't have bothered to wait until the apartment was empty before breaking in and stealing something," said Ware baldly. "Who knows, they might have broken in while you were there just to grab the feather and kill you as a bonus."

Marveaux had been with us on a trip to the Chain of Rocks Bridge a few weeks ago; I knew he was still a bad guy, but the situation was more complicated. He had no love of humans, but apparently had no stomach for opposing Ware, at least right now. It was difficult to tell with these creatures if they were in a mood to kill you, ignore you, or help you, and for what reason.

Castro noticed I was still tense. "What, isn't Fish a friend of yours?"

"I don't think that counts, exactly," I said. "He's been alive since the dawn of time, basically. What's one mere mortal to all that?"

I looked at Ware, who seemed slightly embarrassed by the statement. "That's more or less true," he said, somewhat apologetically. "It can be difficult to really bond with a human when you know they'll be dead in a mere flicker of time."

"But some do," I said, thinking of a few of the stories I'd heard about love affairs between Ware's kind, who called themselves the Forlorn, and humans. "Lucy had that lover a thousand years ago she's still not over."

Ware gave a small nod of acknowledgement.

"Oya and Mia," I said.

At those names, Ware's face darkened. Castro noticed. "What's wrong with Oya and Mia?"

I snorted. "Well, I know what I think is wrong with them, but I believe Ware has a different opinion."

Ware shook his head. "That's neither here nor there. Fish is our concern right now. He has one of his own feathers back. That's not good."

"Okay," I said slowly. "But how bad can it be? Shouldn't you all have feathers around Earth somewhere?"

"No," he said. I was liking this new, informative Ware. "When we agreed to get rid of our wings, and become truly Earth-bound, we destroyed them, down to the last feather."

I remembered the longing of Oya's to have her wings back. "Everyone agreed to this? Knowing you'd miss them as badly as you do?"

"We all agreed," said Ware softly. "Because there were other things to compensate. We knew, one day, we'd get back to our old lives, that the stars wouldn't be put off forever. But in the meantime, our wings were crippling us, not helping us. We cut them off and destroyed them. This feather shouldn't exist."

"But it does," said Castro. "And now Fish has one of his own feathers back. So, what, he wears it as an earring or something? I mean, what's so bad about a single feather?"

Ware pursed his lips together.

"And you were just in a sharing mood," I said. "You might as well tell us. After all, you're the one who's upset Fish has it when you wanted it for yourself."

"I didn't want it for me," said Ware. "I've been trying to collect all the talismans, and store them away where no one else can use them."

"You mean no one besides you," said Castro.

Ware's anger returned. "Of course, no one besides me. I trust myself. I don't trust the others. Any of them could be working for *him*. Lucy's already demonstrated that she's still in his camp. Others may be as well."

I thought for a moment. I didn't necessarily trust Ware with my life, or Castro's life. After all, he was immortal, and we weren't. We couldn't rate very high on his list of priorities. But some of the other Forlorn seemed to trust him over this rival of his, because Ware was more of a laissez-faire boss, while the other guy was much more of a micromanager who wanted to control everything and everyone around him.

Of the two, I suppose I'd trust Ware more. But that didn't necessarily make him trustworthy.

"What can he do with it?" I asked. "Control fire? Change the weather? Bring down buildings?"

"Worse," said Ware. His face paled.

"How much worse?" I asked, fear clawing at my heart. If this could frighten my boss, it had to be scary.

"Worse," Ware said softly. "He could bring back his old form. His old self. One of us, in that form, would be enough to do whatever we wanted with life on earth, including destroy it."

"Destroy it?" I repeated. "Like, he could wipe out all life on Earth?"

"People?" asked Castro. "Animals? Plants? Bacteria even?"

"People," said Ware. "And everything else, too. But most certainly, as of the moment Fish had that feather in his hand, humans were looking extinction in the face."

I sank onto a bar stool. Extinction? At Fish's hands? I couldn't square a word like *extinction* with the low-key barfly I knew as Fish.

The door behind me opened wildly and a cold wind slammed into my back. "Ware!" shouted someone. "We have a problem."

2

I turned around to stare at the owner of the voice. Oya. Also known as Little Girl and Babs.

She was tall, maybe over six feet, with hair so close-cropped she was almost bald. She wore silver bracelets from wrists to elbows and looked as though she could spear someone through the heart without qualm.

My stomach did a slow queasy roll. One of Oya's talents was possession; she could take over the body and mind of certain people. The fact she couldn't do it to everyone wasn't much of an upside. Not when I was one of the few people she had that power over, and that she'd used it on me a few months ago.

Consent was a concept Oya had trouble with. It did not endear her to me.

"We have multiple problems," said Ware evenly. "You are responsible for most of them, I think."

That stopped Oya for a second.

"Or am I wrong in assuming you are here about the pregnancy?" he asked.

Oya shrunk in on herself, almost as if she were a deflated balloon. "My fault," she said with resignation. "I suppose. But..."

"No buts," I said before Ware could get another word in. "That pregnancy is on you." *The conception, too.* That was my beef with her. She'd possessed someone and used his body to make her partner pregnant. If using someone's body against their will, or at least without asking permission first, wasn't the very definition of rape, then I didn't know what was. Jordan wasn't the stablest guy, or at least that was my assessment after meeting him, but having possession and fatherhood thrust upon him without being consulted certainly wasn't going to help him overcome his issues.

Oya was a rapist, no doubt about it. That had her on my shit list.

"I need somewhere safe for Mia to wait out the last few days," Oya said. "The sky's getting darker."

"You knew what might happen," said Ware. "Why should I grant you refuge?"

Refuge? From a dark sky?

"It's not tornado season," said Castro before I could.

"Nobody asked for your opinion," hissed Oya.

I stepped forward and her gaze swung to me. "I don't know what this is about, but you won't speak to him like that. Whatever it is that's your fault isn't his problem."

"What do you know?" she barked out. "The war's coming. We need a warrior on our side that can't be defeated. The Thunderer was prophesied to be the one we needed."

I had no idea what that meant, but it certainly sounded like she was using Jordan *and* Mia to create a child for far more nefarious reasons than Mia simply wanting to be a mother.

"Creating the Thunderer was none of your business," said Ware. "Assuming he would even be someone you could control."

"He'll be my son," said Oya. "I will teach him where his allegiances should lie."

"He'll be Mia's son, too," I said. "And Jordan's. Won't they get a say on how he's raised?"

Oya opened her mouth, then shut it, as if she hadn't given any thought to that.

"The Thunderer is a separate issue," said Ware. "And one that's not as pressing."

"Not pressing?" asked Oya. "He's due in less than a week, and the sky's been rumbling over the house for a month. Lightning's struck two trees in our neighborhood in the past three days. We need to find somewhere to hole up for the birth, or who knows how much of St. Louis might burn down."

"So, your treatment of Mia and Jordan isn't your responsibility," I said, "but it's Ware's to help clean up your mess?"

Oya took one step toward me. Just one.

Before I could say anything, Ware was between the two of us, his back to me. Damn, he could move fast when he wanted. Castro actually jumped back in surprise.

"I'll consider your request about Mia," Ware said. "But only because Mia doesn't deserve this."

Oya bowed her head to him. It always amazed me that someone as tall and clearly powerful as Oya would submit to my boss, who normally seemed just like a medium-height graying white dude with odd white eyebrows tipped in black. He was barrel-chested, broad but not fat, and strong. But most of the time, Ware didn't give off the same kind of vibes as Oya. She looked and moved like someone who was used to power and knew how to wield it.

He, on the other hand, just seemed ordinary. Until he chose not to. Then it was clear that no one else in the room approached him in terms of power. He *was* power. A shiver ran down my spine, from fear or awe, I couldn't tell.

"Now, the other matter we have to discuss also involves you," said Ware. "The feather I sent you for. The one you lost. Teryl found it, and now it's gone."

Oya's gaze went back to me. Her eyes narrowed. "Then how is this not Teryl's doing?"

"She didn't know what it was. You knew, and you had been sent for it. Yet somehow, you lost it. The fact Teryl found it before anyone else could should have been a good thing, but she didn't know to give it to me, and of course, I had no idea she had it. I only knew you had it, and then lost it."

"So, it's gone. Humans lose things all the time," said Oya haughtily. I so wanted to slap that look of condescension off her face. I'd have to jump up to reach, but I'd do it, even at the sacrifice of my dignity.

Ware did slap her then.

"Your fault," he said again. "Yours. She didn't lose anything; the feather was taken while she was doing an errand for me in London."

Oya put a hand on her face and glanced at me sulkily. "So, it was taken. As long as Fish doesn't have it, I'll have it back to you by tomorrow."

The silence that followed was as pregnant as Mia.

"Oh," said Oya. "He has it."

"Here's what's going to happen, before anything else comes up," said Ware. He turned away from Oya and went back behind the bar. "Teryl and Little Girl will go look for Fish. Even if he has his old form back, Little Girl should at least be able to slow him down."

"But I won't have my wings," she said. It was almost a whine, and sounded odd coming from such a tall and powerful individual.

"You have weapons from the old times," said Ware without raising his voice. "Use them."

That perked Oya up. Perhaps Ware had previously forbidden her to use these nifty *old time weapons* and now she had permission to break them out. I had a feeling that Oya with those weapons would be at least as bad as Fish with wings. Or, at least, I hoped so. Though I was afraid, too. Nothing was simple with these creatures.

"Shouldn't be too hard to find him," said Oya with a grimace. "We'll just follow the trail of bodies."

"Bodies?" I asked. "Fish wouldn't kill anyone."

"Fish wouldn't," said Ware, "But Glowing Embers in the Eternal Fires of the Void wouldn't hesitate."

"Glowing *what*?" asked Castro.

"That must have been his pre-Earth name. Or, one of them, anyway," I said. "This one," I pointed at Oya, "was *Sapphire at the Eye of the Storm*, or something like that."

"Something like that," she said, mimicking me. "Our names don't translate well into human language."

"I'm sure they don't," I said, "and I don't care. I just want to know what Fish is likely to do now. Besides kill people, apparently."

"Likely to do?" asked Oya incredulously. "Anything he wants!"

"But what is that?" I asked. "So far as I know, Fish just wants to drink, because it dampens his ability to pick up the thoughts of the humans in his vicinity. His main goal since I met him has been to *not read minds*."

"That won't be a problem as long as he has that feather," said Ware. "He'll be able to read, or not read, any mind in the area. Not just human, but ours as well."

"He'd be able to read your mind?" I asked. That wasn't a wrinkle that would have crossed my mind to even worry about.

"Only with a lot of concentration," said Ware. "It will be difficult for him, and he'd have to be very close, possibly within arm's reach, but he could do it with enough time and effort."

"That doesn't solve the problem of what he wants," I said. "You say he can now do anything he wants? Well, what *is* that?" Honestly, I hate having to repeat myself, but these creatures were going to make me do it by not answering my questions. If they did that to protect me, or just because humans were, as a rule, beneath their notice, I didn't know. Didn't care. Just answer my damn questions.

"Return to space?" asked Oya. "Find a hole to hide in so deep no one can find him ever again, war or no war?"

"Speaking of this war," said Castro, "when is this likely to happen? You all talk like it's going to be tomorrow, but doesn't this other guy have to show up first and recruit an army?"

"He's already recruiting," said Oya. "Notice how you haven't seen Yama and Lucy lately? They're sounding the others out, the ones that agreed to follow Ware's lead after the banishment of his rival."

"But there aren't that many of you," I said. "How long could it really take? A few weeks? A few months?"

"Maybe," said Ware. "But our perception of time isn't like yours."

Another cop-out answer.

"Now, maybe the two of you should start looking for Fish," said Ware. He nodded toward Oya. "No quarter this time. We can't afford to have him loose."

I shuddered. No quarter? That meant we were on a mission to kill.

I'd never killed anyone. Now I guess I wouldn't be able to say that anymore. And I'd have to do it in the company of the woman I currently despised more than anyone in the city.

"Let's go," said Oya.

"Fine," I said. "My car's just outside."

"It's small," said Oya as we stepped outside into the shock of January chill.

"Your problem," I said. "It's my car or nothing. So, squeeze yourself in somehow."

It was a measure of how cowed she was by Ware, or by whatever Fish would do with his feather, that she said nothing.,

I would have preferred a snarky remark. That I could have coped with. Her silence was more frightening than any other response she could have given.

3

I drove down the street to the first stoplight before I realized I had no idea where we were going.

I drove a few more blocks, made a left turn on Washington, and just cruised the city for a few minutes to see if Oya would start giving directions.

Which she did not.

I made another left turn, which put me facing south. From here, I could see the copper roof of St. Louis University Hospital.

I almost made another turn, which would have had us moving back toward the bar, but I was tired of Oya sitting in my car saying nothing when she was the one who knew more about the situation than I did.

"So," I said. "Do we turn? Where are we going?"

"Home," she grumbled.

"Whose home?"

"Mine, of course," she said. "I need to get my weapons. Fighting Fish won't be easy."

"So start giving directions," I said. "I only know you live somewhere near Lafayette Square. Also, what kind of weapons work against your kind? I thought you couldn't be killed. Except that one person that one time."

"She's not really dead," said Oya. "Not in the sense you mean it, anyway."

I shook my head. "Too complicated for me. Now, what about these weapons?"

She snorted derisively. "You want Ware to tell you everything, but the moment things start getting difficult to understand, you shrug it off as *too complicated.*"

I wasn't sure that was fair, but maybe it was. I needed to know more about these creatures if I were going to survive their war, but the truth was I didn't want to know. *Need* and *want* are entirely separate things.

"Oh, crap," said Oya. "You have this stupid thing in your car? Hasn't it eaten the wiring yet?"

I heard the low chirp that meant my pet scrap, Cookie, was annoyed by something. Probably Oya's feet.

I glanced over quickly, deciding I would take Grand southward and wait for Oya to give me actual directions. In the meantime, I could find a bit of amusement that the imposing goddess sitting in my passenger seat was nonplussed by the presence of Cookie in the car.

Cookie was a small brown thing that looked like a cross between an origami vampire bat and a gnome. Sort of. It was difficult to peg what it actually resembled because the mind refused to grasp it for long. No matter how long I stared at Cookie, memorizing its features, the exact shade of brown of its skin, the delicate tiny claws and the needle-like teeth, I couldn't keep a terribly accurate picture of it in my head.

Cookie was currently clutching the back of the passenger side headrest, sniffing Oya's head and humming tunelessly to itself.

"No, it hasn't eaten the wiring," I said. "And it goes where I go, even when I have to stuff it in the luggage for an overnight flight." Cookie had ridden out the trip to London in my checked bag. Fortunately, things that were dead did not need oxygen.

"You should get rid of it," said Oya.

"Oh," I said as if I were interested in her advice. "You have a weapon for killing scraps? Things that are already dead?"

"Even the dead can die," said Oya so pretentiously I almost laughed. But I swallowed down the laughter because, despite how weirdly funny that sentence was, I knew she was serious. Death wasn't necessarily the end, and if Cookie were any indication, what came after was not necessarily any better. It could be worse.

Cookie was a dead human, but not just any human. A human like me, like one of the Lost. Those humans who had a touch of Forlorn ancestry and could sometimes have some of the powers of that race. Regular humans couldn't become scraps. Humans like me could. Cookie was a reminder that death might mean, for me, another life as a simple-minded little papery goblin creature. Something so insignificant it was a *scrap*.

Something a being like Oya might stomp out of existence just for being too near her.

No one looks forward to death, at least not without some super super good reason like being in intractable pain from a terminal illness. But for me, death wasn't necessarily going to be *death*. Which made me think it was probably preferable to whatever fate I was going to get instead.

"Turn right," said Oya, bringing me back to the situation in the car, and the errand I had been sent on.

"So, fill me in," I said as I turned where Oya had indicated. "If Fish has his feather back, what are we going to be dealing with?"

Oya made a grunting sound, at me or Cookie, I didn't know. "We'll be a disadvantage. He should be about as invulnerable as it gets. Like, bullet proof times a thousand."

"He's already pretty invulnerable," I said. "I saw him get shot in the gut, and when I saw him next, which was a couple of days later, he seemed completely fine."

"Sure, a gunshot isn't going to kill any of us," said Oya. "But it can hurt a lot, at least for a few hours. If he has his feather, the bullet's liable to bounce off of him and he won't even notice the sting. Something as insignificant as a *bullet* isn't going to even get his attention."

"But you have weapons that will get his attention," I said.

She hesitated, then shrugged. "Maybe."

Oh great.

Oya continued giving directions, and I, for the most part, ignored her except for following those directions. She wasn't someone I wanted to be around, and now she was as bad at keeping information to herself as Ware had ever been.

It didn't take long for us to arrive in the vicinity of Lafayette Square. But I would have known we were close just by the atmosphere.

Dark clouds loomed overhead, but only over an area of a few blocks. The clouds were occasionally illuminated from within by lightning. It was like a sky billboard announcing something supernatural.

"Surely this is getting reported on the news," I said in awe, and a little bit of terror. "Mia's baby is doing this?"

"I think they're calling it a weather anomaly or something," said Oya. "I haven't paid that much attention. If I can get Ware to take Mia in, the neighborhood can go back to normal."

"And if Ware doesn't?"

Oya pointed to a spot along the street where I could park. I pulled the car over.

"If he doesn't, then I have no idea what will happen when Mia gives birth," said Oya. "No one really knows the Thunderer's true powers."

"How do you even have a name like that for this kid? Or is that a title?"

"It's a prophecy," said Oya, which made me groan. More prophecies?

"Wait, I think I know how this story goes now," I said. "Zireya, the one who died, the one who managed to have a child with a human, the one Ware and his BFF both loved, the one who could tell the future, at least sometimes, said something about a child being born who could cause thunder."

"She said war would happen again, and it would destroy worlds if no one could stop it. Only the Thunderer would be able to bring the universe back under control once...once the war started."

This was starting to sound like that weird prophecy in *Star Wars* about some child bringing balance to the Force, and then everyone thinking it was going to be the guy who ended up as Darth Vader.

"Prophecies never seem to turn out well," I said, realizing Oya wasn't saying all she knew once again. I'd heard the catch in her voice and wondered what she had been going to say before amending her statement to merely end with *once the war started.* "I assume Ware thinks you're an idiot for forcing the issue."

I got out of the car and Oya unfolded herself out of my tiny hatchback. "We need as much help as we can get," she said as she slammed the door. "This is important. Ware has to see that."

I looked up at the angry clouds, which were dark gray mixed with green. That was a sickening color that always seemed to come with tornado sirens attached.

"Let's get inside before you get hit by lightning," said Oya. She walked up the steep concrete steps that led to the giant Victorian mansion that she and Mia apparently called home.

The three-story behemoth was painted a pale green with dark green shutters. Its walkway was made of some kind of stone; I had no idea what it might be. Marble? It wasn't concrete, anyway. The portico above the front door was held up by four pillars that still had green bunting strung between them, though Christmas was a month behind us now.

The windows had electric candles in them, which were turned on and gave the place a beautiful glow. I spotted a few red ribbons still tied to the wrought iron fence that surrounded the property.

It would seem this household had decorated for the holidays and hadn't remembered to take anything down.

I guess the advancing pregnancy and danger from stray bolts of lightning had distracted the residents.

Oya opened the door and stepped into the house. I followed more slowly, unwilling to face either Mia, who seemed sweet but had been complicit in the rape of Jordan, or Jordan himself. I didn't know how much Jordan knew, or remembered, about what Mia and Oya had done to him, or if he'd been told and reconciled himself to the news, or what. If it had been me, I was sure I'd have walked away from the pair and never looked back. But he was living here with them. I didn't know how that was possible, and wasn't sure I wanted to know. Mia, Oya, and Jordan had to work that out between them, and the less I knew, the better.

4

The front room of the house was a warm yellow with white trim. Unlike the outside of the house, the inside had no obvious holiday trappings, being festooned instead with decorative plates and dark wood furniture. The artwork on the walls seemed to mostly feature European cities under gray skies. To me, even one painting of a city enduring gloom and rain would be too depressing to live with, let alone several hanging in the same room. Somehow, the drab artwork managed to bring down the cheeriness of the wall color, giving the overall impression of sadness and melancholy.

Or maybe that was just me reflecting my own anxiety back at myself. Here I was on an, oh, *angel-hunt.* Forget about humans being *the most dangerous game.* The Forlorn were worse. I didn't have to have any experience in hunting the Forlorn to know this was true.

Mia came into the room from the back of the house. Her face lit up when she saw Oya. "What did he say? Can we leave? Will he protect us?"

Oya walked forward and hugged the smaller woman. Mia was shorter than me, which made her probably a foot shorter than Oya. Mia's blond curls were as I remembered, but her face was rounder. In fact, it wasn't just her belly that had grown with this pregnancy; every part of her seemed to have ballooned out to an awkward, and possibly unhealthy, extent.

"He hasn't agreed yet," said Oya reluctantly. "I'm here to pick up a few things and go out again."

"An errand for Ware," said Mia flatly. She did not approve of Oya leaving her on Ware's business, that much was clear.

"This shouldn't take long," said Oya.

Mia pursed her lips together but said nothing. Oya kissed the top of the shorter woman's head and went into another room. I heard a door open and the sounds of someone going down stairs. I guess Oya kept her weapons in the basement. Mia's hands went to her expanded abdomen.

I was going to assume they had a birth plan that accounted for situations in which Oya was home, and when she was not, and leave it. Not my business how Oya and Mia shepherded this kid into existence, especially since it seemed they were aiming to create some kind of superweapon in the shape of a child.

I spared a brief stab of pity for the kid, and nodded at Mia. She nodded back. Her eyes were tired, the bright blue of their irises seemingly dull with fatigue.

"Not too long now, I take it," I said, making small talk as best as I could. It wasn't one of my talents.

"Maybe a week," she said. "At the most. I swear, he's planning to kick his way out."

A tall man came up behind her. Whereas Oya's skin was almost flat black, Jordan's skin tone was slightly lighter, more a warm chocolate than cold jet.

He had lost weight; when I'd seen him last summer, he'd been much rounder, though not enough to be fat. Now he looked more trim, if not athletic. He was holding a hammer in his right hand; his left arm ended just below the elbow. A war injury, I'd been told, from a tour in Afghanistan.

The other thing that was different about him was his demeanor. When I'd seen him last, he was clearly disturbed by his previous experiences with Mia and Oya. Now he appeared relaxed, almost peaceful.

"Hello," I said. I gestured toward the hammer. "Fixing up the house?"

"Working on the baby's room," he said.

He said nothing more, which did not surprise me. He hadn't said much the last time we'd met; he seemed reserved. Whether he had been like that before he'd enlisted, I didn't know. From what little Mia had let drop about him, it seemed Afghanistan had changed him significantly. This Jordan was not the same Jordan who had been a fling of Oya's before his enlistment.

The fact he looked happier and more fit meant he probably wasn't the same Jordan I'd met a few months ago. Maybe he'd come to terms with what Oya and Mia had done. Maybe incipient fatherhood meant something to him, no matter the circumstances of the conception.

I didn't want to continue to think about that, or I'd be too angry to let Oya back in my car.

I had no idea what to say. Mia just stared at me with ill-disguised resentment, and Jordan stood behind her, as mute as the furniture.

"Check on homicides in the area today," shouted Oya from a distance. "We're going to be tripping over a lot of bodies if we don't get a handle on this now."

I had no idea who she was talking to. Should I whip out my phone and search for *homicides St. Louis past 24 hours* or something?

But Jordan apparently assumed she was speaking to him. He gave a little nod and walked out of the room.

"Homicides?" asked Mia. "Why is Ware concerned about dead humans?" She walked to a chair and sank down into it. Her face was pale and drawn and she appeared exhausted.

"Should I get you something?" I asked. "Like water?"

Mia shook her head. "No, no. I'll be fine."

I stood, fidgeting, and wondering how much longer Oya was going to take. I was also curious as to what kind of weapons she would be bringing with her on this little escapade.

Meanwhile, I was stuck here, shifting my weight from foot to foot while Mia glared at me from across the room.

The strange stand-off continued for several minutes until Jordan came back. He had a few sheets of paper, which he held out to me.

"Here," he said. "Creve Coeur Lake, earlier today. Two people killed."

I took the papers, glad of the opportunity to look at something besides Mia or the room's depressing art.

Jordan had printed out a report about two people who'd gone out to the lake early in the morning to hike, which seemed ridiculous to me considering the outside temperature, but then, some people seemed to like the cold. In any case, the two people had reportedly been about halfway around the lake when something ran out of the woods. One witness described it as a tall broad crazed person with a knife. Another thought it was some kind of bear with long claws, although they described the bear as more red than brown.

Fish had always been a tall, lanky guy, at least in my acquaintance. His clothes hung loosely on him and his shoes had holes. Everything about him seemed worn and old. He'd never looked strong enough to lift a ten-pound weight, much less be mistaken for a bear or a crazed person with a knife.

I supposed he could have been wearing a red fur coat or something. Or maybe there was a crazed murderer on the loose, and it had nothing to do with Fish at all.

I heard the thumps of someone coming up the stairs and the sound of a door closing. I was relieved. Though I hated the cold, being in this house was even less pleasant than being outside.

Oya walked into the room carrying a satchel. It wasn't big enough to hold a sword or a rifle. Would we be going after Fish with a knife, or a pistol, or dart gun? Or maybe we'd just tase him?

"All right," she said. "Let's go. You have a location?"

"Two murders, Creve Coeur Lake, this morning," I said, waving the papers in her direction. "Is that the lead you wanted?"

She nodded. "Let's hope we can keep this to two murders. Otherwise, the body count will simply grow until we get this under control."

"How do we know this was Fish?"

She frowned. "I guess we don't. But the scene of a double homicide is a good place to start looking for him."

I turned and walked to the front door. I didn't know why every Forlorn had immediately jumped to the conclusion that Fish would turn homicidal if had possession of the feather, but they knew their species better than I did. If two murders were the best-case scenario, then I didn't want to know the worst.

5

The police had the park at Creve Coeur Lake cordoned off. Apparently, it had been long enough since the murders had been announced that the media and whatever other immediate looky-loos had come and gone. That meant I could drive right up to the cordon. The uniformed man at the cordon frowned at us as I stopped the car.

Oya merely stared at the park intently. Could she sense another of her kind in the area, perhaps? Or was she glaring at the police officer through the windshield until she cowed him with her intensity?

"I need to find out the condition of the bodies," said Oya at last. She opened the door and unfolded herself to get out of the car. "Stay here."

"Absolutely," I said. Cookie made a quizzical noise and hopped up into the front seat recently vacated by Oya.

"I don't know what difference it makes," I said to the papery thing. I put a hand on its withered shoulders. Cookie looked up at me and cooed. I smiled at it, surprised that I had taken to the thing so quickly. "I guess she'll tell us what she thinks we need to know," I said, including Cookie in the *we*.

Oya towered over the officer, of course. She towered over nearly everyone. I don't know what she said to him, but he said something back to her, rather sharply. I heard his tone, but couldn't distinguish the words.

Oya was apparently satisfied. She came back to the car. I herded Cookie to the back seat, which did not make it happy. It made a disparaging snort but obeyed.

"Well, we're too late," said Oya. "But I think we might have a lead on where to go next."

"How does any of this make sense?" I asked. "What could you learn here that helps us find Fish?"

"The bodies were ripped apart," said Oya baldly. "But in a precise, surgical way."

"Like what supposedly happens to cows when aliens experiment on them?"

Oya looked at me with disbelief. "Mutilated cows? What are you going on about?"

"Never mind." I said it dismissively but it occurred to me that, in this case, it was true. If Fish had mutilated these people, they had indeed been dismembered by an alien. If two people weren't dead, it would be funny.

"Let's go," she said. "To the Chain of Rocks Bridge."

"Really? The bridge?"

Oya didn't bother to answer. I put the car in drive and slowly pulled out into the road. The bridge wasn't far from the park, but as a destination, it seemed an odd choice. The bridge was where Ware had hidden the entrance to some pocket dimension he had created and now controlled.

"What would Fish want with the bridge?" I asked. "That's kind of, like Ware's personal territory, right?"

"Yes. Think of it as the announcement of a territorial fight. Fish will want to collect anything useful Ware has in his possession. And Ware doesn't keep the good stuff in the bar."

I sighed. "So, Fish can't do whatever he wants unless he gets some of Ware's stuff?"

Oya shook her head. "No, he can pretty much do whatever he wants. The thing is, we all gave up a great deal when we got rid of our wings and bound ourselves to this planet."

I pulled the car onto 141 and drove north. "And?"

"And it's not so easy to just leap out into space again after ages here on Earth. It can be done, but he'll need to get some energy."

"Is that why he's now murdering people? He's eating them?"

"More or less."

"More or less? So, is he removing organs or drinking their blood or something? Are you guys the inspiration for angel *and* vampire legends?"

"Maybe. Sure. I suppose we could be the inspiration for vampires. It's irrelevant, though. He's sucking out these people's, well, souls. The things that turn into scraps when you die."

"But that only works with the Lost."

"True. He'll take the soul of one of the Lost if he can, because you have more energy. But the souls of normal people, that usually just rather dissipate after death, are there for the taking."

"And the mutilation part? Couldn't he just, I don't know, strangle them? Does he have to rip them apart?"

"The mutilation's just for fun," she said without hesitation or, apparently, any awareness that this was a horrific thing to say. Fucking fallen angel piece of shit.

Indignation and anger welled up in my throat. But I cut it off. If I started screaming about things now, I'd be a mess by the time we actually got close enough to Fish to kill him. I needed to keep a handle on things. No panicking.

I wasn't sure I'd be able to do that, but I knew I'd have to.

Cookie seemed to sense my mood. It clambered onto the headrest behind me and chirped in my ear.

Oya ignored it, but I was heartened by its loyalty. I had a feeling I was going to need any support I could get.

"We're in this together, bud," I said to Cookie. "Promise."

Cookie just chirped again and licked my ear.

I kept the car going north. The bridge was only a few miles away. What would we find when we got there? My heart beat against my ribs as I feared I would not even be able to imagine what we would find.

No matter what I thought or suspected would be there, I was sure it would be much, much worse.

6

The parking lot by the Old Chain of Rocks Bridge had been blocked off with concrete years before due to an excessive amount of vandalism that had occurred there with sad regularity. I had to park at the Visitor Center a half mile away so that we could hike over.

Just what I wanted to do: hike in the frigid late January temperatures.

I had no sooner gotten out of the car than I heard the sounds of sirens in the distance. The sound rapidly grew louder. Shit.

"More deaths?" I asked.

"Maybe," said Oya, though she sounded more certain than the word would normally indicate.

"Look," shouted a child who was just now running out of the Visitor Center. The kid looked thrilled and pointed toward the bridge.

I turned around and stared at the black smoke that now billowed from behind the leafless trees in the direction of the river.

The Mississippi River had flowed through this channel for thousands of years; it had cut the continent in half since at least the end of the last Ice Age. The bridge, of course, was much younger. Part of the original Route 66, the bridge had seen crime, historic travel, Hollywood film crews for the movie *Escape from New York,* and now the presence of supernatural creatures and pocket dimensions tucked within its girders.

I'd read up on the place after I'd been tossed off the bridge in an encounter a few weeks ago between Ware and his allies, and Rakes, which, it turned out, were not an internet creation, but very, very real.

"What's burning?" I asked, a bit stupidly, I guess.

Or, at least stupidly in Oya's opinion. The gaze she leveled on me was scorching enough to catch *me* on fire.

"Whoever Fish has murdered lately," she said. "Or something else flammable."

I turned my thoughts away from the vision of burning bodies, and thought about anything else that might be used to make a fire. "There's plenty of driftwood around," I said. "It doesn't have to be people."

Again, the withering glare.

"Oh," I said. "Because a blood sacrifice is required or something? He can't just set something on fire like wood or paper?"

"Something like that," she said.

Cookie hopped up on the car's hood and peered at the smoke. It made a grumbling noise and wrinkled its nose. I guess the scrap could smell whatever was burning from here.

Something flashed just behind the treetops.

"Those first responders are in for a surprise," said Oya calmly.

"We should warn them," I said, suddenly realizing that Fish must still be in the area. "He'll kill them, right?"

"Probably," said Oya. She seemed more resigned than worried. "But at least we know where he is."

"Then we need to get to him before they do," I said. "Let's go." I started walking in the direction of Riverview Drive, which was the only way to access the bridge from the Missouri end.

Oya laughed. "You think you're going to do something against Fish? Even in his dissipated barfly shape, he's more than a match for a human. Now, he's a god."

"Then I guess you'd better come along," I shouted over my shoulder. "So your goddessness can kick his god ass. You got weapons. Use them."

Cookie jogged along beside me. I had no idea why it clung to me so closely, but its loyalty was heartwarming. It seemed to have little fear, though I knew it could be killed. I'm pretty sure I'd killed one in my very first encounter with the Forlorn, when I had to rescue Castro from two immortal fuckers who wanted to use his soul to open a portal to another dimension.

At least, there had been a squirming something in a sack. I'd thrown the sack at one of the Forlorn, and in the ensuing explosion of light and power, whatever had been in the sack had been destroyed. At the time, I had no idea what it had been. Now I was almost positive it had been a scrap.

I glanced at Cookie. Now that I had a better idea of what a scrap was, and even had one as a kind of uncomfortable pet, could I do that again? Sacrifice something to win a battle? Especially if it were something I cared about?

"Are we just supposed to walk past the first responders?" I asked. "I don't think they're going to want to let us onto the bridge, assuming that's where Fish and his newest victims are."

"They might stop you, but they won't be stopping me," said Oya haughtily. "Few people are willing to get in my way."

I wanted to roll my eyes at that, but I didn't. What would that help? Honestly, I'd originally found Oya intimidating, so I got it, but now that I'd found out how little our moral compasses aligned, intimidation had turned to disgust.

As I thought, we were stopped as soon as we crossed Riverview Drive and approached the blocked-off parking lot. A police officer held up a hand. "Either cross the street or go back," he said. "You can't come any closer right now. This is a crime scene."

"What's going on?" I asked. I didn't bother trying to hide Cookie. For some reason, most people seemed unaware of it. Not that Cookie was invisible, more like human brains simply refused to process the information that a small dead thing was standing at their feet.

The officer glanced at Oya, then back at me. I suppose he wasn't really supposed to talk about what was going on, but he seemed freaked out and eager to talk to someone, anyone, about what had happened on the bridge behind him. Oya pushed the situation by looming over him and staring pointedly.

"Three people, looks like they got dropped from a height," he said. "Like, how do you even do that? Can drones pick people up these days?"

"I don't think so," I said.

"And then, I mean, it's so weird. Their eyes are missing. Their tongues. Maybe more things. It's not possible for your eyes to just pop out of your head, right? And your tongue? Ain't gonna happen, no matter how far you fall." He shivered, but I didn't think it was from the cold. "My mom always talked about Satan walking among us. I never took her seriously. But this...this is something else. Maybe she was right."

"Satan doesn't exist," said my companion, who was likely to have been the inspiration for plenty of religious figures.

The officer shook his head. His face was paler than the cold winter day would account for. Whatever he'd seen had really freaked him out.

I could sympathize.

"Is that it?" I asked. "Just three bodies dropped out of the sky onto the bridge? Three bodies missing some organs?"

"Isn't that enough?" he asked.

I didn't want to say *yeah, that's awful and tragic, but not humans-will-be-wiped-off-the-face-of-the-earth stuff.*

"Did anyone see who did it?" asked Oya. "Or did anyone report something strange flying by?"

"What, like a flying saucer or something? You think aliens did this?" asked the officer. He sounded like he wanted to be skeptical, but he didn't have the heart to be just now. Whatever he'd seen, it was too weird for him to simply accept it as being within the bounds of what he considered reality. Yet he really, really wanted it to be. "I heard something about flashes in the sky. Maybe a reflection of a balloon or something?"

He seemed to be fishing for any kind of explanation that would help him sleep tonight. Again, I sympathized. This was crazy, and awful, and goddamn stomach-turning, and wasn't going to get any better. Not unless Oya and I succeeded in somehow subduing or killing Fish.

I looked into the steel gray sky. A passing eagle flew north. As hard as I looked, though, only ordinary normal Earth things were in view. The trees, the clouds, the steel trusses of the bridge.

"Perhaps we should go," I said. "If there's nothing more to learn here."

Oya seemed reluctant. She glanced around, as if something were going to jump out from behind a tree and yell "gotcha!"

"He was here not so long ago," she said. "Maybe ten minutes."

"Does that mean he's close by?" I asked. "How quickly can he move?"

"He who?" asked the officer. "You know who did this?"

"Bear," said Oya quickly. "We're on the trail of a bear. Like the one that was captured in St. Charles County last summer."

"Never heard of a bear around here," said the officer. He started to turn but all at once, he was simply gone and the sky was filled with a horrendous shriek that didn't come from a human throat.

I was so startled, I literally fell backward onto the ground. Oya drew a knife and raised it above her head.

I blinked, tried to slow my breathing, and stared upward. Now that I was looking, the form of the police officer hovered several hundred feet in the air. He screamed and struggled, but what held him was strong and implacable.

What held him was horrific. It looked like a cross between a person, a metal dragon, and a crystal chandelier. Light bounced off its many planes and angles, making the forest around us sparkle as if a giant disco ball were above us and not a homicidal monster.

Large wings that were the darkest red, yet also shiny and reflective, spread out on each side of the creature. Once again, it threw back its head and let out an inhuman wail.

The police officer was dragged through the leaden skies toward the bridge, and then unceremoniously dropped. He missed the bridge and disappeared from view. At this distance, I couldn't hear him hit the water, though he no doubt had.

Distant shouts rose from the bridge; the other officers had noticed their comrade falling out of the sky. Whether or not they'd spotted the monster over their heads, I did not know.

Oya started forward. "Come on," she said. "He's distracted by the police. While he's picking them off, maybe we can get close enough to do some damage."

"So, shouldn't I have a knife, too?" I asked.

Oya held out a blade barely longer than a paring knife. The metal was purplish and reflected light oddly, as if it were covered in a strange oil.

Hell, maybe it was.

"Here. If he gets close to you, aim for the eyes. Or the wings. Forget about a body blow; that won't damage him enough to slow him down."

I followed the tall dark image of vengeance toward the bridge. My heart was either going to smash through my ribs, or climb up my throat; it did not appear to have decided which.

Cookie growled as it loped along at my side. We were a ridiculous combination to be going into battle, especially as back up to Oya, but I guess that's what we were.

On the bridge, another shriek. Fear shot through me all over again.

I'd liked Fish. He'd been one of the most easy-going of these creatures. He'd been pitiful most of the time, too. Now, he was something else again. Something deadly. Something far too alien for the mind to even want to contemplate.

And I was headed right for him.

7

More screaming from the bridge caused Oya to break into a run. I thought for a moment she was hurrying with the idea of saving people.

"Do you think any of them will still be alive by the time we get there?" I gasped in between deep breaths.

"He'll be distracted," she said, as she hurried on ahead.

I had no chance of keeping up with her, so I slowed and finally switched to a fast walk, one hand pressed against the stitch in my side, while I sucked air into my lungs over and over to try to catch my breath. Fucking bitch. She didn't care about the people who were being attacked; she only cared that Fish might not notice her approach while having his fun killing people.

A terrifying screech came from right above my head. I looked up and there was Fish, or what Fish had become.

His great wings bent and beat the air around them, jointed mostly like a bird's, but angling oddly from his back in a way no Earth creature's wings ever had. His hands were outstretched; each finger ended in a golden talon that somehow glinted in the weak winter light.

Instinctively, I stretched the blade Oya had given me above me, waving it about overhead. My heart sank as the creature I used to serve alcohol to at the bar ignored it and dropped down closer to me.

Suddenly, Cookie screeched and launched itself into the air. It leaped maybe twenty feet into the sky and grabbed Fish's hand.

The frightful monster Fish had become was unconcerned; it shook the scrap off and continued its descent.

I swiped at its hands, and tried not to obey the instinct to run. Run where? As soon as I lowered my hand and the knife, he'd be on me, and I'd be flung through the air to fall on the bridge, or into the river.

He'd kill me the moment I turned my back.

"Fish!" I shouted. "What do you think you're doing? Why are you killing people?"

Cookie leaped up again and swiped at Fish's foot. This time, Fish swatted the scrap with a wing, and Cookie hit the ground with a thud.

"Teryl! Run!" shouted someone. Oya.

I couldn't look away from Fish to see how close she was. Running wasn't an option and she had to know it. I had to keep this horrific thing from grabbing me until she could do something about it.

I tried not to think about how these things couldn't die, except maybe that one time, except that hadn't really been true death. No, I couldn't kill him, and I couldn't run. The best I could do would be to survive the next few seconds.

Small bits of concrete began streaking past me toward Fish. Cookie. It must have found some place where the parking lot's concrete had broken down in to small pieces and was still trying to defend me.

A flash of purple smacked Fish on the side of the head. Fish screeched and shot up into the sky. Whatever had struck him fell down a few yards from me and made a metallic clang against the remains of the parking lot.

"Why didn't you run?" shouted Oya as she drew up beside me. "You can't hurt him."

"Run where?" I shouted back. I waved the knife she'd given me in her general direction and I was gratified to see her back off. Maybe this weapon could harm any of the Forlorn, no matter what form they wore. That was heartening. I didn't trust them, and now I had a weapon that might help me against them, should I ever have to stand against one or more of them.

Not that I knew how to handle a knife as a weapon. I glanced around nervously but couldn't spot the bright metallic figure of Fish anywhere in the sky. He was gone.

Oya's face was a combination of fear and anger. "What would Ware do if you got hurt?" she asked. That explained the fear. Not fear of me, or Fish, or the situation, but fear of Ware.

"What does it matter?" I asked. "Fish is still out there killing people. How many this time? Five? Ten? More? How do we stop him? Has he left just to collect more people to drop onto the bridge?"

"Killing random people isn't working for him," said Oya. "He's going to try something else. He might start going for the Lost. If you're protected, there's..."

"Jordan," I said. Jordan had never told me he was one of the Lost, but Oya had told me those were the only people she could possess. And, well, if that were true, and she'd possessed Jordan, the arithmetic wasn't that hard to add up.

"I should never have left him behind," she said.

My phone rang. I literally jumped.

"It's Ware," said Oya. "Answer it."

How she knew who was calling was beyond me. But I didn't doubt her. Maybe he was able to send her a telepathic message that he was calling. How would I know?

I pulled the phone from my pocket and answered. "Yes?"

"Get back to the Angels' Share," Ware said.

Oya heard and shook her head. "I've got to get home to protect my family."

"They're here," said Ware, who had clearly heard her. "So, get here as quickly as you can."

"All right," I said. I didn't bother to tell Oya what he'd said since she was obviously eavesdropping.

Oya was uncharacteristically subdued as we made our way back downtown. I pulled into the alley behind the bar. The truck that had been at Oya and Mia's house was already there. Must be Jordan's.

The moment I had the car parked, Oya was out the door. She opened the back door of the bar and was inside before I'd even turned off the engine and gotten my door open.

Whatever. I didn't care to be around her, anyway.

I stepped into the cold and clutched my coat around me; the alley was pointed in just the right direction to funnel winter's worst stiff breezes right down one's collar.

A scream from above me made me jump backward. I looked up. Fish flew overhead; he must have followed us. Not that this was such an unusual place for him to be: if he wanted talismans or other objects of power from Ware, and couldn't get into Ware's sinkhole at the bridge, then the bar was the next best place to come.

I grabbed at my pocket. The knife was there, right? I didn't feel it. Damn, where had I put it? In the car? In my other pocket?

Fish dropped to the pavement in front of me. His strangely angular face was disturbing, as if it were composed of multiple planes of broken glass that were simultaneously dark and on fire. My brain was screaming at me to run, but I managed to hold my ground. There was nowhere I could run that would be safe from a fucking immortal extraterrestrial that was made of crystal and metal and could fly.

"Fish," I said breathlessly. Between the cold and my terror, it was hard to speak. My throat was tight, my jaw clenched in fear and the bracing cold that made my teeth hurt. "Fish, you don't have to keep hurting people."

He made no indication he understood. He merely took a step nearer me and cocked his head as if deciding in which order to remove my organs.

There. In my left pocket, not my right coat pocket. The knife. I grabbed it and held it out.

Fish leaped toward me, but I held the knife out in front of me. "Come on, fucker," I shouted. "Come and get it. I'll gut you with this. I swear it."

The back door of the bar flung open so hard it slammed against the side of the building. Ware's barrel-chested form leaped into the alley; his right hand held out in front of him. He screamed something in a guttural language that was clearly not meant for human throats.

Oya followed him out, along with another Forlorn, Truck. As per usual, Truck looked like a denim-clad biker complete with bandanna around his forehead, scraggly beard, and silver chain attached to a belt loop and ending in a pocket.

Fish leaped backward but didn't fly away. Even confronted with three of his fellow aliens, including the most powerful individual of their kind that I was aware of, he did not seem unduly worried about the odds.

That made me nervous.

He should have been nervous himself, surely. Oya was intimidating enough but Ware, when he chose, was even more intimidating. The sense that this man was more powerful than anyone else in the room smacked you in the face when Ware chose to unleash his abilities.

Fish was unimpressed. He screeched again, but this time added a few guttural sounds of his own. Unlike the strained sounds coming out of Ware, the guttural noises were beautiful and harmonic coming from the crystalline and metal form of Fish.

"Get inside," said Oya as she moved between me and Fish. "Stay with Mia and Jordan. We'll hold him off."

I turned and ran, not comforted by the *hold him off* phrase. I would have preferred something more permanent like *we'll get rid of him* or *we'll disable him*. I couldn't count on *we'll kill him* since they insisted death was impossible for their kind, but at least one of them had still *died* somehow. Why not make it two?

I found Mia and Jordan in the bar. Jordan had his right arm around Mia's shoulders.

"She's okay, isn't she?" asked Mia.

She? Oh, she meant Oya.

"They're all fine, as far as I know," I said. "And I'm okay, too. Thanks for asking."

Mia frowned. "I can already see you're all right," she said. "But when Oya said Fish had followed you here..."

"She knew?" I interrupted.

"I guess she saw him flying overhead," said Mia. "Like far enough up that a human wouldn't see, but she could."

Well, it wasn't like Fish hadn't known where the bar was, or where we were likely to go. What difference did it make that Oya had seen him, but hadn't let me know?

I grabbed a tumbler and an Elijah Craig from the shelf and took the bottle with me to a table. I poured out a generous portion of the amber liquid and looked around for Castro.

Jordan and Mia were the only other people in the room. "Where's Castro?" I asked. Surely he wasn't in Ware's office, or a closet. Toilet?

Jordan didn't even look at me. Mia shrugged. "He said he had something important to do. He called for an Uber a while ago."

I nearly dropped my glass onto the floor as my heart leaped painfully against my ribs. "He what? He *left*? And you let him?"

Jordan said, "Ware said as long as you and Oya were keeping Fish busy at the bridge, it would be safe for a while."

Mia just folded her hands in front of her on the table and stared at them. From outside, I heard a shriek and then the rolling peal of thunder.

We had three problems: a monster flying overhead with murderous intent; a pregnant woman carrying some kind of prophesied super soldier; and my boyfriend off somewhere in an Uber.

I picked up my phone to call Castro.

8

Castro didn't pick up.

"Hey," I said as soon as the phone went to voice mail. "Where are you? Why did you leave the bar? Get back here right now, or let me know where to pick you up."

Me leaving probably wasn't a good idea, but at least I had a weapon of a kind. I might not know how to use it, but I had it. I had to believe Fish would try to kill me, assuming he had the chance to, and he was still feeling murdery. But he might be distracted for a while; I had no idea what was going on in the back alley between him and Ware, Oya, and Truck, but it might be useful to sneak out while he wasn't paying attention.

Except my car was in the back alley, too. So that precluded a sneaky exit.

I could call Uber just as well as Castro could. I contemplated doing just that. But before I could call them, my phone rang. It was Castro.

"Where are you?" I asked without preamble. "Why did you leave the Angels' Share?"

"Petunia," he said. "I couldn't leave her in the apartment for Fish to find. He'd probably eat her or something."

"Wait, what?" I asked, stunned. "Why would he be interested in a hedgehog? He's been killing *humans* all day. I doubt Petunia's on his radar. Plus, you going back to the apartment might have given him the opportunity to follow you, except he was following me and Oya."

"That's what Ware said. So, see, it works out," he said. "I'm headed back. I sent the Uber away now that I can use my car."

"Hurry back," I said. "Fish is fighting Ware, Oya, and Truck in the back alley..." I stopped speaking as I heard the back door swing open. Truck clomped into the bar, followed by Oya.

"Ware?" I asked, my heart inexplicably in my throat. Fish couldn't harm someone as powerful as Ware, could he? As much as I mistrusted my boss' motives sometimes, that would be very bad, because in this war everyone seemed convinced was coming, his opponents' motives seemed even more suspect.

Not to mention a homicidal angel flying around the city picking people off at will wasn't a good thing. I was sure Ware would be needed to cope with this.

Oya nodded. "He's all right. Fish is gone for now. Ware's sent your scrap to the roof to draw some protective runes up there."

Shame raced through me as I realized I'd forgotten about Cookie until now. It was loyal to me, but I'd completely let its well-being slip my mind.

The back door opened again and this time Cookie rushed in and jumped into my lap. It chattered at me as if delivering the story of what had happened in the alley and then looked at me as if requesting approval.

"Um," I said. "You did good." I petted it on the shoulder. It glanced at Ware briefly, its paper-thin ears going back for a second. It shuddered. Whatever Ware had gotten it to do outside had frightened it, it seemed.

I hugged it a little tighter, both weirded out by how protective I felt toward it so shortly after I'd failed to worry about it all, and pleased to have something to care for.

I shook my head. This was all too confusing. A strange itching started behind my eyes and I rubbed them. Stupid jet lag.

"Castro left," I said to Ware. "He said you said it would be all right."

"He wanted to go and there wasn't going to be a safer time," said Ware. "As soon as Fish turned his attention away from the park and the bridge, things were going to get dangerous again."

As safe as possible wasn't very safe. I felt like saying that out loud, but for one, I managed a tiny bit of discretion. Still, I was afraid for Castro's safety, especially now that he'd been warded off by Ware and his runes.

"Did you make contact with any of the others?" asked Oya.

Ware shook his head. "Can't find Pellagrio or Marveaux. We already know Yama, Lucy, and Mink will support Isya when he comes. The only ones we can depend on are in this room."

I frowned. I was sure Truck was loyal to Ware, and Oya always had been in the past, from what I'd been told, at least. But would her loyalty hold if Mia were threatened? Or the baby? I doubted Oya cared that much for Jordan, but the others? She might very well betray Ware if he didn't protect them.

"Castro's on his way back," I said. "When he gets here, what are we going to do to keep everyone safe?"

"The runes on the roof will ward Fish off for now," said Ware. "They'll fade over time and we'll have to get a bit more drastic."

"Take Mia to the sinkhole," said Oya. "Protect her."

"No," said Ware. "No one's leaving here now."

Oya glowered at Ware, but the slump of her shoulders signaled her obedience to Ware's will. Maybe her loyalty was still strong.

Truck said, "You got any food here, Ware? We may be able to go without food, but the humans can't. Mia certainly can't."

Ware shook his head. "I don't keep food here."

"I'll get some," said Truck. "If Fish thinks he can get the better of me when I'm on the watch for him, he'll need to think again."

"Fine," said Ware. "Just come back as quickly as you can."

"Remember that Castro's coming," I said. "So, there'll be four humans here, not three."

Truck just nodded. He walked out the front door, giving a look to the sky before striding off. The door swung shut behind him, giving a dull thud that sounded ominous in the current situation. Maybe everything was going to look or sound ominous until Castro was back.

I took a deep breath and just hoped he could get here soon. I didn't really think we were terribly safe here; Ware's assurance that the runes would work, but that their protection would fade, was hardly reassuring. On the other hand, being near Ware was likely to be safer than anywhere else.

It's just that *safer* didn't necessarily mean *safe*.

Oya's insistence that Mia be ensconced in some kind of pocket dimension only accessible by Ware led me to believe that even she wasn't convinced the wards on the roof would work well enough to keep those she cared about free from harm. So how could I be confident of my safety, or Castro's?

Cookie hopped off my lap and began moseying around the bar, sniffing every stain on the floor. Disgusting, but at least it kept Cookie occupied.

The itching behind my eyes sharpened. I squinted and pressed a hand to my temple. Stupid to have started drinking alcohol while jet lagged. Even I, who was hardly a world traveler, knew that the air on planes was very dry and dehydration was something to consider after a long flight.

I got up and grabbed a glass from behind the bar. I filled it from the sink and went back to my table.

"Are you all right?" asked Ware.

I shrugged. "Jet lag. Dehydration. The usual post-long flight problems people have."

Ware nodded, but his gaze seemed wary, as if he felt I were trying to cover up something. I couldn't imagine what that would be. Why would I bother to lie? What did I even have to lie about?

The spike behind my eyes stabbed me and I gasped in surprise and pain. I squeezed my eyes shut and put my head on the stained bar table.

Something tugged on my pants' leg and whined. Cookie. It gave a sharp bark.

"I know," said Ware.

I heard him sit next to me, but the rising pain in my head kept me from looking over or even opening my eyes.

The beer-and-cleaning fluid scented table underneath my nose was the only thing keeping me from collapsing onto the floor. As the pain lurched upward, I groaned and plastered my hands to the sides of my head as if I could keep my brain, which seemed to be threatening to explode out my temples, where it belonged by willpower and the force of my palms on my skin.

"He's still here," someone said.

Various creaks and groans sounded around me. Every sound speared its way into the center of my head through my ears and I screamed.

Rustling. Then more rustling. Footsteps. I couldn't make out any meaning to them; they were merely sounds that punched their way through my skull. Every one of them was horrifically painful.

And then the pain transformed. It was still horrible, but now, inside my head, I saw something inside the pain. A vision. The pain beat around it, but the vision itself was sweet and clear.

In the vision, I soared through a vast multi-colored universe of light. Colors I had never imagined swirled around me, clinging to my wings as if attracted to their fiery beauty. My heart soared to the sounds of stars singing their names into the vastness of space. The bliss I felt seemed to go on forever, and I didn't want it to stop. Not ever. I wanted to feel this way as long as the universe lasted.

But that did not keep the chaos I now sensed behind me at bay, and I understood I was fleeing something. Something terrible.

The song of the star behind me was suddenly snuffed out. Panic rose inside me; the war was too close. I had waited too long to flee.

Something caught the tail edge of my right wing and I spun around. The being that had grabbed me was beautiful, shining purple and blue with silver accents. Sapphire at the Eye of the Storm, wholly loyal to the being I now glimpsed behind her.

His wings reflected the light of the stars so brilliantly, he was difficult to look at. He was silver and white made even more blinding by the light of the galaxy caressing his wings and reflecting from them languidly as if reluctant to leave him. Light had always seemed to be attracted to him. He was fire and light and brilliance and desire and will wrapped in a crystalline form that shone so bright. Light loved him; it slid along every plane and angle of his wings like drops of silver. Beams of glorious white light caressed his hands, his face, his feet.

He brought light where previously there was only darkness. He was the Lightbearer. He was beautiful, almost as beautiful as the creature at his side.

She was crystal that reflected all colors; she was brilliant blue and yellow and green and orange. She was the largest of us with a wingspan far broader than any other. No one who saw her failed to be captivated by her, consumed with the need to be close to her, to bask in the multi-colored points of light that flickered off every plane of her body and wings. As much as light seemed to cling to the Lightbearer, it leaped off of her in rainbows of glorious exuberance and joy.

She was alluring and captivating and more terrifying than almost anything in the universe. She was Wholeness. She was Creation. She was everything wondrous about our race made manifest in a single entity.

I had been a fool to think I could escape her or the Lightbringer.

And then...a smashing cold hit me and I was suddenly aware of being in a heavy lumpy human body that most assuredly did not travel between the stars on wings that reflected starlight.

"She won't thank you for that," said someone.

"Teryl? Teryl?"

I knew that voice. It was...my boss. Ware. I blinked slowly and realized the horrible pain in my head had vanished, leaving me feeling woozy and hung over, but at least human.

I lifted my head slowly and glanced over at the broad figure of my boss, whom I had just seen in his own form. *"Lightbearer,"* I whispered.

"Guess you were in Fish's head just as much as he was in yours," said Ware drily. He rubbed his left palm with his right thumb as if the palm were stinging with pain.

I was suddenly aware that my right palm was stinging. I looked at my hand groggily. The red brand on my palm, the design that I had been told was Ware's own name in his kind's own script, burned and itched.

"I got him out of your head," he said, eyeing me with what appeared to be both admiration and misgiving. "It wasn't easy; Fish has always been the strongest of us when it comes to piercing the privacy of another's mind. But it's rare for the one he's attacking to have the wherewithal to attack him back."

"Attack?" That sounded ridiculous. These were immortal beings whose fits of temper demolished *worlds*. No human could attack one.

"You saw his memories," said Ware. "That's unusual. Normally, Fish can look into another's mind without revealing his own thoughts. It takes a very strong mind to take advantage of the bridge to invade his mind while he's invading yours. The strongest." The words seemed dragged out of him.

"But that means while I was seeing some random memories of his, he was seeing inside my head," I said. "What could he have found out?"

"Anything," said Oya. "Social security number? Computer passwords? Your favorite food? He could take whatever he pleased."

I frowned. "I can't imagine what he'd want to know. He already knows where I live. What good could my social security number do him? I don't have enough money in my checking account to tempt anyone to steal from me, but what good would money do him, anyway?"

"No, he wouldn't need money," said Oya. "Don't be ridiculous."

I glared at her, wishing I could make her submit the way she always did to Ware.

"You're all looking at the wrong thing," said an unfamiliar voice. I glanced over at the booth where Mia and Jordan sat. Jordan was looking at the rest of us with contempt.

"What would be the right thing, then?" asked Oya before I could.

"Castro," said Jordan. "He left here, so he's unprotected until he gets back. Teryl knew that, so Fish knows it now. He'll be looking for Castro."

My heart sank. "Shit. And he knows what car Castro drives. If Castro were still in an Uber, Fish might not find him so easily, but in his own car, he'll be obvious to Fish." I looked at Ware, hoping that wouldn't be true. After all, there were lots of little blue hatchbacks out there.

Ware only nodded, though. "He'll know the route Castro is likely to take. He knows the car. It won't be hard for him to grab Castro."

Fear took my breath and I struggled to breathe. All over again, I saw the cop snatched into the air from in front of me, and then plunging toward the river to his death. That would be Castro.

For all I knew, Castro was already dead.

"I have to go," I said. I stood quickly and lost my balance. Ware caught me before I could hit the floor. The room spun crazily.

"You need to sit down until you regain some equilibrium," said Ware. "You've had Fish in your head. That will take a bit of time to get over. I doubt he was very delicate or kind in his sifting of your thoughts."

"Who cares?" I asked, pushing against Ware's chest, and now terrified of what it meant that Fish had been in my thoughts. "Let me go. I have to get to Castro."

"How do you propose to do that?" asked Oya. She looked down her long nose at me. I had never wanted to strangle her more than in that moment. "He'll be driving toward downtown, and you'll be driving away. It's not like you can just wave him down. All you'll be doing is making sure you're both in danger."

That made sense. I didn't care. "So what? I can't just sit here and wait to receive news that his car was run off the road by some weird winged creature."

"That's exactly what you should do," said Oya.

"Is that what you would do if Mia were in danger?" I asked.

Oya's eyes narrowed.

"Right," I said. "You'd do anything to keep her safe. But you'd tell me to sit here and just wait."

Ware gently pushed me back toward the chair I had been sitting in. "It's best if you wait here, but I will go out and look for Castro. Little Girl will stay here and protect you, Mia, and Jordan. Truck should be back soon so you'll have two of us, plus the wards on the roof, to protect you."

Cookie jumped onto the table and gave a disgruntled bark. Ware didn't even give the scrap a glance.

"Yes," I said. "Two Forlorn, runes on the roof, and a scrap. We'll be as safe as we can be."

Ware shook his head. "I can't believe you take that thing seriously.

Cookie hissed. I tapped on the table to distract it. Getting Ware angry with it wasn't a good plan.

Cookie chirped and hopped off the table to lean against my right ankle. It looked up at me with a satisfied smile.

Ware sighed. "Right. I'll be off."

Something thumped on the roof.

I closed my eyes and gripped the edge of the table. It didn't take much imagination to think that Fish had just dumped Castro's body where we'd be sure to hear it arrive.

Ware and Oya leaped up.

"Stay here," he said. "We'll take care of this."

The two of them went to the back and the door banged open.

I couldn't keep the tears from flowing. Castro. What would I do if Fish had harmed him?

I hoped desperately that the noise on the roof didn't mean anything bad had happened to Castro. Hope and fear warred for supremacy in my heart.

Cookie jumped into my lap and I hugged it to my chest and waited for news.

9

Ware came back fairly quickly. He held a small plastic box. It took me a moment to recognize it as the kennel Castro and I used to transport our pet hedgehog Petunia when she had vet visits.

"Petunia?" I put Cookie down and got up. Ware put the pet taxi on the table in front of me. I didn't want to look inside; could a little body like hers survive a fall onto the roof of this building?

"She's fine," he said. "A little bruised maybe, but fine."

"What about Castro?"

Ware was silent, and my heart nearly stopped. Then he shrugged. "I don't see any evidence of him around here. If Fish has him, he has him somewhere else."

"But he must have him," I said. My heart started beating again but it was in my throat. My temples throbbed in time with those beats. "If he went home to get Petunia, then she was in the car with him. If she's here, and he's not..."

Cookie hopped onto the table and sniffed at the pet taxi. It wrinkled its nose, which it had never done to Petunia before. Its nose twitched quickly and it glanced around, stared hard at me for a long moment, then ran toward the back of the room and squawked.

"What's up with that thing?" asked Oya. "Can't you control it better than that?"

I frowned. Cookie's motives were generally a mystery to me. I had no idea what a dead person, one in such an alien form and without language, might want. But it seemed obvious to me what Cookie was looking for in this instance.

"I think I'm supposed to follow it," I said.

"What, it's a bloodhound now?" Oya laughed out loud. She clapped her hands together, which made the silver bracelets she wore clang together.

Rustling sounds came from the pet taxi. I don't think Petunia was happy with the chiming of Oya's bracelets. Of course, I doubt Petunia was happy with anything right now. I wanted to somehow let her know it would be okay, but I didn't know that. Nothing would be okay if Castro were hurt or dead.

"I don't know what it freaking is," I said as I tried desperately to control my fear. "You guys are the ones who are supposed to know about things like scraps. But I think it wants me to follow. Maybe it caught Fish's scent from the kennel."

Oya snorted derisively. "That thing might think it can track Fish, but it's just a scrap."

"And Teryl's just a human who somehow got into Fish's head," said Ware. He appeared thoughtful.

"Look," I said. "My car's in the alley. I'll go with Cookie and see what I can find out. I'm going to go out looking for Castro no matter what, so if following a scrap's nose is the best chance I've got of finding him, then that's what I'm going to do."

Ware glanced at Cookie, then back at me. "I could keep you from going," he said, but he didn't put any force behind it. It was more a statement of fact.

"If you want to keep me here, you'll need to tie me up or knock me out or something," I said. "I'm going. No discussion."

Ware nodded. "I'm going with you, then. Little Girl and Truck can hold things down here."

"Where *is* Truck?" asked Oya. "Shouldn't he have been able to get some food here by now?"

"He'll be back soon," Ware said. "When he returns, just let him know we're out looking for Fish and Castro, and that he's to stay here with you, Mia, and Jordan."

He looked at me. "You'll need something to defend yourself with."

"I have something."

Ware looked skeptical and glanced at Oya. "You gave her a weapon?"

To my surprise, Oya looked chagrined. "Well, sort of."

"Sort of?" I pulled out the knife she'd given me and laid it on the table.

Ware picked it up and pulled the blade out of the sheath. "At least it's real," he said. "But too small and not the best she has." He tossed the blade onto the table, which made Cookie hiss from its spot on the floor near the back wall. "What do you have on you that will work?"

Oya protested, "I'll need my blades to protect Mia and the baby."

As if the skies were listening, a crack of thunder pealed through the air. Mia grimaced and put her hands on her abdomen.

"He's kicking," she said. Jordan tightened his grip on her shoulders and she leaned against him.

"You've got more than one knife on you," said Ware. "Don't ask me to believe you don't. In fact, I see the handle of one sticking out of the waistband of your pants. Hand it over."

Oya stiffened. "That's the only *ziferenya* I have. The other blades are adequate, but not nearly as good."

"Fine. Then Teryl will have the best. Hand it over." Ware's voice was unemotional, but it was clear he wasn't taking *no* for an answer.

Oya tried to keep Ware's eyes but only for a moment. Once again, her shoulders slumped and her gaze dropped. I didn't know how such a powerful creature as Oya could be so cowed by Ware, but I was glad this was going to work out in my favor.

Oya reluctantly pulled out the knife, which had a black handle and sheath. She held it out slowly.

"Thanks," I said as I took it. The blade was heavier than the one she'd given me earlier. I pulled the knife slightly out of the sheath.

The metal that was revealed was so brilliant as to be almost white, but the metal itself had a distinctive ripple pattern that reflected the yellowed beams of the overhead lights in a similar way to how light had reflected off of the crystalline wings in Fish's memories. My eyes were dazzled by sparkles of blue, orange, red, yellow, green, and violet. A rainbow of radiance nearly blinded me.

"Zireya made this," said Ware. "Most have been destroyed over the ages. This knife is more ancient than you can imagine."

I refrained from saying something sarcastic; after all, if I could imagine the Big Bang, then I ought to be able to imagine that the blade could be millions, or even billions, of years old. But it wasn't important. Castro was. If this blade made his recovery even slightly more likely, then I was going to carry it around on me until I got him back.

I ensconced the blade back in its sheath. "Let's go," I said. "Who knows what Fish is doing to Castro."

"Assuming he still lives," said Oya. I turned away from her, doing my best to hide my panic and my disdain for her. She didn't have to take low shots like that, even if she didn't like me or Castro. She still knew I was frantic to find him.

"Cruelty doesn't become you," said Ware.

Oya said nothing to that. She wouldn't talk back to the Lightbearer, even now. The shreds of Fish's memories that remained in my mind echoed the sentiment. Sapphire at the Eye of the Storm had always been the right hand of the Lightbearer, even before the war. Nothing had ever come between them.

Not the war. Not Isya. Not even Zireya.

I shook my head and started to walk out.

"One moment," said Ware.

I turned to him. "What?"

"I have a few, um, weapons of my own," he said. He ducked into the door marked Private, the one that led to his office behind the bar.

Cookie jumped up and down in impatience. I sympathized. I was ready to go, but if Ware thought he had more weapons to be used against Fish, then it was probably good for him to fetch them.

It didn't take long. Ware emerged from the office with the kind of stiff black bag that doctors in movies always seemed to carry. He nodded to me and we went out the back.

Cold wind slapped me in the face as soon as we got into the alley. It was carrying large fluffy snowflakes, the kind that are heavy and will make a horrific mess of the roads.

"Fuck," I said. "This will make it harder to get around town."

"Then let's not delay any longer," said Ware. He got into the passenger side of my car without a single comment on how tight the fit would be. He kept his bag on his lap.

Cookie, who was used to the passenger seat, didn't hesitate to hop in the back without even making a single squawk. It would seem Ware intimidated even the dead.

"Okay," I said as I turned the engine over. Nixie, my car, was pretty good in the snow, but I hated to drive in bad conditions, because other people would be doing stupid things.

Ware didn't put on his seat belt; I guess being an immortal being meant he didn't necessarily have to worry about the long-term effects of any crash we might have due to other people's idiocy.

Cookie was already dead. So, no worries there.

I, however, was very much alive, and mortal, and wanted to rescue my boyfriend, not end up in the hospital. I clicked my seat belt and looked over at Ware.

He sighed. "I don't know where Fish is, but I think, after the fiasco at the bridge, he'll want to head for more familiar territory. We'll go to his place."

That was the first time anyone ever mentioned Fish had "a place," though I suppose of course he had to live somewhere. I just couldn't imagine where that would be.

"So...." I asked with raised eyebrows.

"Not too far," he said. "He lives in an apartment just off of Forest Park Parkway, near DeBaliviere."

That placed him in the Central West End, the place where one went to experience sidewalk cafes and upscale stores that probably preferred to be called *boutiques* or maybe *shoppes*.

But it was arty, too. Someone like Fish, who always looked mussed and unkept, as if he had stayed up too late drinking and writing poetry, wouldn't necessarily stand out.

I headed west. The journey wasn't far, just as Ware had said, but traffic would probably delay us a bit. I tried to tamp down on my impatience. I wanted to slam on the accelerator and rush to the Central West End as quickly as possible.

Snow kept my mind on the roads, which were, at the moment, mostly slushy. They would freeze tonight into a mess tomorrow unless the city's salt trucks and snow plows could tame it into submission.

I didn't trust the city on that account, but at least that was the future. For now, I just needed to make sure I didn't do anything rash, like stomp on either accelerator or brake or twist the steering wheel too quickly. Slushy roads weren't too bad, but could be treacherous if you weren't careful.

The trouble was, other people weren't always careful. I'd barely gotten two blocks away from the bar before the first near-accident occurred. An elderly lady in large sedan slid through an intersection after trying too quickly to come to a halt.

Fortunately, I was able to stop and let her slide by in front of me.

Ware said nothing; he seemed almost too calm, especially considering we were going up against one of his own kind who had transformed back into a flying powerful, basically supernatural, creature.

Well, Ware was supernatural, too, but now Fish was *really* something alien and powerful.

"So, what kind of things is Fish capable of now?" I asked. "Besides flying and homicide, I mean."

"Well, clearly, he can get into your head," said Ware. "But it looks like you can get into his, as well, so he might not try that trick again."

"How common is that?" I asked. "For people to be able to turn Fish's tricks back on him?"

Ware hesitated, then shrugged. "As you know, we all have our gifts...powers. I can make sinkholes, control scraps, and use my name as a weapon. Fish is telepathic and can manipulate fire. Lucy can do the same things Fish can do with fire, but with water. Mink can also control scraps. But the ability to block a power, or to use it against someone, that's...rare."

"How rare?" My stomach clenched in anticipation because I knew what he was going to say.

"Only one of us could do that, and a human? Never."

I waited a moment, but he was reluctant to say. Fine. I'd say it.

"Zireya. My many times great-grandmother."

A long sigh seemed to force its way out of Ware. "Yes."

Clearly, he still wasn't over her.

"How long has it been? Since she...died."

"Thousands of years," he said.

"And how long since you came to this planet?"

Another sigh. "Thousands of years before that."

"And doing that, coming here, losing your wings, that was Zireya's idea."

"Yes."

"Why?" I thought about the vistas of space I'd seen through Fish's memories. The stars had been like friends, each one singing its own song. The paths between galaxies had been lined in light and darkness, both the darkness and light equally beautiful.

What could make a being that could soar in between galaxies and drink in the starlight want to come to one tiny corner of the universe, lose the ability to fly, and wander the planet in heavy fleshy bodies of blood and bone?

"We needed...sanctuary," said Ware at last.

"From the war? From each other?"

"No," he said in a strained voice.

He said nothing else, so that was apparently all the information I was going to get today. Still, it was a start, and it was more than he'd said to me about him and his kind in, like, *ever*.

I should be glad to have a little more information, but I guess learning about the past wasn't what I needed right now.

"More important," I said, "is what are we going to do with Fish once we catch up to him? Can you cast a spell on him, or shout your name and pummel him with the sound or something?"

I could almost hear my boss rolling his eyes at me. "What? Pummel him with sound?"

"Well, you can use your name as a weapon, right? So, you shout your name at him, and, what, it drives him off?"

"That's not what that means. I can't even say my name properly with a human throat. But I can write it in our script. You already know that."

Yes. He's used a marker to scribble some kind of rune on my hand. He'd thought it would be temporary but after I'd bled on it and used it to attack another one of Ware's kind, it had been branded permanently onto my body. Into my soul, if you believed what the Forlorn had to say about it.

"Could you draw it on yourself?"

He didn't answer right away.

"Or is that a secret?" I asked.

"I...I never considered it before," he said at last.

"You didn't consider whether it was a secret?" That was me: about to go to war with a terrifying alien creature and I couldn't keep myself from saying stupid annoying things to the one guy who could probably keep me, and Castro, alive.

"You know what I meant," said Ware evenly.

"Sorry," I said.

"It's fine," he said. "I've known you were a sarcastic bitch since I hired you. It's hardly a surprise. And, no, I never thought about drawing on *myself*. I don't think it would work."

"Why is that?" I asked while watching another car slide through an intersection. This one wasn't as close as the lady from the previous intersection, so my heart rate managed to stay level.

"It's hard to explain. Could you make yourself stronger by wishing the strength in your left arm would transfer to your right arm? Something like that."

"Except you guys are, like, magic. I have no idea what you could *wish* and have it come true."

"Magic isn't real," he said. "Make sure you're in the right turn lane up here. The apartment complex isn't far away now."

"Any idea if we can find out if Fish and Castro are here before we get too close?" I asked.

In the corner of my eye, I saw Ware's hands tighten on the bag in his lap. "I don't think we have to worry about that."

"Oh shit," I said, as I pulled the car over. Flashing lights blocked the road ahead and someone was allowing one car at a time to get by.

"I guess we know that someone saw something alarming," said Ware.

I wanted to say something to that, but my heart was in my throat. What if what someone had seen was Castro's body?

"Let's go," said Ware. He got out of the car.

Cookie immediately jumped into the passenger seat and chirped at me, as if giving me encouragement.

"Yeah," I said. "Let's go. We've got to get him back."

Cookie cooed and hopped out of the car. I followed, my feet as heavy as lead, and almost immediately frozen by the three inches of slush in the street.

But who cared about cold feet? I had a fiery alien to fight in order to get my boyfriend back.

Assuming he was still alive. I trudged forward through the slush and around all the stopped cars. I kept my eyes on Ware's back and walked toward our appointment with a homicidal being I used to consider a friend.

10

A policeman tried stopping us as we neared the apartment building. He held up a hand and spoke to Ware.

"We have a situation here, sir. You'll have to go back."

Ware didn't acknowledge the man, just kept on moving. The officer frowned and started to say something, then seemed to forget Ware's existence and turned to look at the stopped cars on the parkway.

I walked by, keeping my eyes downcast, and waited to see if I could benefit from this weird sort of invisibility. The officer let me go by. I wasn't surprised he let Cookie go by without discussion; most humans seemed incapable, or perhaps simply psychologically unwilling, to see it.

The apartment complex was painted a dull gray and had white trim that was equally dull. The overall appearance was neat, but merely functional. No expense had been put into making the place seem inviting or friendly. Maybe the owners of the complex figured the neighborhood was hot enough to get people to move in without them having to apply any attractive décor, landscaping, or anything that would improve the curb appeal.

It was hardly the sort of place I would have thought Fish would visit, let alone live in. He seemed like the sort of guy that would have either rented a tiny loft with two other, equally disheveled-looking people, or he would be in some kind of substandard unit where the plumbing perpetually leaked and people went to sleep to the constant strains of the neighbors screaming at each other or their kids.

Ware seemed familiar with the complex. He passed two buildings and the first staircase on the third. He got to the second staircase and began climbing the steps; I followed as well as I could, but my shoes were soaked with slush, which had made my feet so cold they ached painfully and each step seemed to jar even more pain through every bone.

Ware went to the top floor, which was the third. I slowed down for the last flight, out of breath and weary of breathing the frigid air.

Cold just made a person exhausted and miserable. I felt like I'd never be warm again.

Ware went to the door labeled 378 and turned the knob. I was sure I heard a strange sound of metal-on-metal before Ware shoved the door open. Guess it didn't matter if the door had been locked.

I knew I probably shouldn't follow but I was right behind Ware. "Castro?" I called out as soon as I entered. "Castro!"

Ware searched the apartment in moments and turned to me. "Not here," he said.

I glanced around. The apartment interior was like many generic apartments: walls of white, floors of dull beige carpet. The one accent was a brick wall to the right. The place was musty with a pervasive smell of alcohol. Considering how much Fish drank, that wasn't surprising.

Cookie sniffed in the corners, but did not seem to be tense. It was only me who was desperate to find Castro; Cookie was just along for the adventure. Or because it simply liked to be where I was.

The furniture consisted of a few plastic chairs, the sort that normally lived on patios and porches until they finally cracked and fell apart from multiple hot summers and frigid winters. A small radio sat on an orange crate turned on its side.

Straight ahead was a tiny kitchen. I went to it and opened drawers and cabinets. Empty, except for a single fork in one drawer. The refrigerator was full of bottles of whiskey. So was the small pantry.

I couldn't figure why Fish would have stuck whiskey in the refrigerator.

The single trash can was full of empty bottles.

I walked down the short hallway past the single bathroom and looked into the lone bedroom. It contained a couple of sheets laid out on the beige carpet.

Fish wasn't living large, except for the whiskey, and I'd bet he'd gotten a lot of that from Ware.

The same thought had occurred to Ware. He picked a bottle out of the pantry; the bottle shape and the label told me it was The Macallan; the deep amber color told me it was an 18-year. Not cheap stuff. Definitely over three hundred a bottle; maybe closer to four.

"I was wondering where that bottle went," said Ware. He put it on the counter and turned to me, a look of disappointment on his face. "I'm not sure where it's best to look next. And I don't want to waste any more time."

"Maybe we should ask the police why they're here," I said. "Maybe someone saw, you know, something weird. Something they couldn't explain. If they saw it going a certain direction, at least we'd have a clue."

Ware looked pensive. "Maybe. But humans generally have a difficult time describing things they don't understand. And they're terrible eyewitnesses."

"Yes, but what other lead do we have?" I said, as tears threatened. "If Castro isn't here, where is he?"

Something thumped up on the roof. Ware instantly tensed and put down the bag. He unzipped it steadily while never taking his eyes off the ceiling.

"Fish?" I asked quietly.

Cookie hissed.

Ware nodded. "Be quiet."

A low growl came from outside. Not from the front of the apartment, but the back. I looked through the tiny kitchen and this time took notice of a door. The apartment must come with some kind of small deck out back.

A shadow passed in front of the door and something slammed into the back wall of the apartment.

The noise shocked Cookie into a sharp bark and it leaped backward, ears flattened against its head. It cowered on the floor.

A loud crash sounded and Ware threw himself between me and the shards of glass that suddenly seemed to have targeted me. I ducked and turned, trying to cover my face with my hands.

Something screamed a high throaty wail that seemed half-crazed with despair, half-triumphant.

Ware said something that wasn't in English. Something thudded on the floor nearby.

I turned and saw the bloodied form of Castro now stretched across the carpet just on the other side of Ware.

"Castro!"

I would have leaped toward him but Ware held up an arm and barred my way. "Don't," he said.

"I have to get to him," I said, though I didn't try to get around Ware. Mostly because the maroon-and-black nightmare angel wings that now nearly filled the room were terrifying. My heart urged me forward; my feet were frozen to the carpet.

The wings weren't soft and fluffy; these were strangely metallic looking, shiny, and sharp. I watched in horror as a few trailing feathers were dragged across Castro's face and left razor-thin cuts.

Reluctantly, I followed the line of the wing currently cutting Castro back toward its origin on the shoulders of a hulking creature that looked like a nightmare cross between a dragon and a lion. Feathers, if indeed that was a better term than scales, covered its face, and spread out behind it like a mane or the hair of an '80s rocker. The feathers rippled and moved as if independently controlled by the horrific creature they were attached to.

The thing had inky black sunken eyes and a mouth full of long jagged silver teeth. Its limbs were long and ended in blades that would have put Freddy Krueger to shame. The whole creature throbbed in time with some kind of weird respiration that made whistling noises in the dry artificially-heated air.

It wasn't exactly like the forms I'd seen in Fish's memory; perhaps this form was something of a cross between what he had looked like in those days and the human he had been for the past unknown number of millennia.

Fish nudged Castro's body and Castro moaned. My heart nearly stopped with both terror and relief. He was alive. Fish hadn't killed him.

But he could still kill him in an instant with those razor-sharp feathers.

Ware took a small step to the right, blocking more of my view of Fish. He once again made a guttural sound and then coughed. I suppose he was finding out just how hard it was to make some kind of approximation of their ancient language with a non-metallic, non-crystalline throat.

Fish tapped Castro with a weird paw-like foot that looked much a bird's. As he did so, he tilted a wing in my direction.

Ware hissed, as did Cookie.

"What?" I asked.

Fish growled; the sound was as if someone were scraping a stone across a steel brush. Despite the metallic nature of the sound, it still held a tone of an organic nature. The impossible construction of the beast was still that of a *beast*, something alive, even if a form of life that had not developed on this planet.

Ware unzipped the bag he'd been holding and, with a sharp barking sound, threw it at the creature.

A small grayish brown creature flew out of the bag and landed on Fish's face. It was the scrap from Ware's office.

Could something like Fish be stopped by something like Cookie? That seemed extremely unlikely, yet Fish threw himself backward and ran into the half-wall that separated the living room from the kitchen area. He couldn't pluck the scrap off his face because of the long blade-like fingers. I was reminded of the character of Edward Scissorhands and how he hadn't been able to do ordinary things because of the blades that made up his appendages.

The scrap shrieked and bit at Fish's face while holding on to his thin, needle-like teeth. Ware took the opportunity to grab Castro's form and pick it up. "Let's go," he said. "He won't be distracted for long. We've got to get out of here now."

I opened the door, desperate to see how badly Castro was hurt, but understanding the need to get away quickly.

Cookie raced out the door and back to the steps, jumping up and down in impatience. I moved as quickly as I could; surely Castro's thin form wouldn't be enough to slow Ware down significantly.

We reached the bottom of the steps before we ran into some officers, one of whom was yelling at us. "What were you doing up there? What's going on?"

"Don't go up there," I said. "Don't! It's...it's..." I could hardly say something like *there's a demon up there* or anything similar. But claiming Fish to be a crazed human wouldn't keep the officers here on the ground.

A terrible shriek rose from behind us followed by another crash. I didn't look back, just kept going in the direction of the car as quickly as I could.

"Watch out! It's got wings!" shouted someone.

Fuck. Fish was already on our trail, and the car was still over a hundred yards away.

"Get Castro to the hospital," I said. I reached into my pocket, found my keys, and stopped to turn toward Ware. I shoved the keys toward one of his bloodied hands. I didn't dare look at Castro too closely or I'd start sobbing and be useless. It was bad enough that the blood on Ware's hands was Castro's. And the blood on the carpet. And on the stairs. And on the ground.

He was losing far too much blood.

"Get him help. Now." I drew out the blade Oya had given me and raised it toward the fiery red creature overhead that was even now twisting its wings behind it as if preparing to dive.

11

Fish's horrible new form screeched as he came for me.

I held up the blade. "Come and get it," I shouted. "You coward! You hurt people who can't hurt you back. Well, come for me and I'll cut you!"

People around me screamed and ran. I heard someone yell "Get down on the ground and..." The voice sounded afraid and didn't finish the sentence. Well, what could you say?

Fish swerved to the side and I swiped at his outstretched taloned feet with the blade.

He turned in midair unlike anything real should have been able to. Did physics not apply here?

Fuck it. I darted forward and jabbed the blade at him. I apparently surprised him, because I drove the blade in between two of the feather-scales on his side.

He screamed and flung himself backward, pulling me along with him. I didn't dare drop this blade or I'd be defenseless.

He fell to the snow-covered ground and I landed on top of him. I tugged on the blade and rolled aside. It wouldn't budge. Quickly, I sat up, put my feet against his hip and pushed against him as hard as I could.

The blade came out of his side and Fish rolled away from me. I struggled off the ground to get to my feet, holding the blade out in front of me.

The blade was red now, and the alien blood smoked in the frigid air.

"Get away from it, lady!" shouted someone.

"Stay back," I shouted back. "He'll kill again if he can."

I held the blade out again, but my arm shook from the cold now. Falling onto the heavy wet snow had sent cold water down into my shoes, and had drenched my jeans. My hands were so cold, keeping my fingers wrapped around the handle of the blade was becoming more difficult. The blood also made it slippery.

I switched the blade into my left hand, wiped my right on my coat and switched the knife back. At least I had a slightly better grip now.

Fish sprang into the air. Cookie jumped up to try to grab him, but Fish was too quick for the scrap. A swoosh of dark red wing knocked the scrap aside.

"Get down!" shouted someone.

A loud crack split the air. Gunfire. I dropped to my knees. I heard Cookie hiss off to my right. No doubt the scrap was gearing up for another grab at Fish.

My attention was on Fish, though. I hoped the bullet could at least hurt him a little. But Fish didn't even seem to notice.

"Bullets aren't going to help," I shouted. "Get away, and get everyone else away."

In the distance, I briefly saw my car pull out in front of other cars, make an undoubtedly illegal U-turn, and speed off. Castro would be safe assuming he could live long enough for help to patch him up. Barnes-Jewish Hospital wasn't that far away; his odds should be good.

"Hang on," I whispered, wishing he could hear me.

The momentary distraction was enough for Fish. He leaped forward, grabbed me around the waist, and took off.

My breath was knocked out of me briefly because of his tight grip and surprise. The ground fell away as the great wings beat the air around me.

The creature holding me, the one I'd served alcohol to every shift for months, when he'd looked human, was as hard as glass, yet I felt the ripple of muscle under the exterior armor. My mind screeched *alien* at me and I shuddered at more than the cold. It was weird how this strange metal-and-glass form caused a visceral reaction in my as soon as it touched me. Seeing it was horrific enough; being *touched* by it was infinitely worse.

Despite the wings, Fish didn't move like a bird. Instead of beating the air in tandem, the wings seemed to twist, twirl and flow around me in a way that was unnatural and somehow terrifying. The world seemed to swirl around us, with the snow both binding me and making me dizzy. I couldn't judge how high we were, or how fast we were going, or in what direction. I only knew we weren't on the ground.

And that I was very, very cold.

My hands felt frozen and almost numb. I managed to slip the knife up the sleeve of my coat's left arm. I didn't let go of the handle, but I wasn't convinced I would be able to maintain my grip much longer. At least I'd still have the knife on me, though.

Provided it didn't slip out of my sleeve.

Stop it. Had to think more positively. I would have this knife. I would pull it out at some point, and I would gut this awful creature. Even if he couldn't die, he could be hurt.

I was willing to hurt him. The strength of my desire to hurt him scared me. I had never wanted to cause another creature any pain before. Not even that nasty dog that had tried to bite me every time I walked down the street to elementary school. I'd been afraid of the dog, and wished it wouldn't lunge at me, but I had never wanted to hurt it.

But Fish? Right now, the only warmth left in me was my anger. Fish had killed people. He'd hurt Castro so badly I had no idea if he'd even survive. And he'd done it deliberately. Maybe that was what got me the most. He'd broken into my apartment when I was out of town because he knew, or at least strongly suspected, I had his feather. He'd come to steal it and use it, knowing full well he'd turn into this...this...*monster*.

I could never forgive him for that. I could have been sympathetic that he'd missed the stars, or that he'd yearned for his lost wings for thousands of years, and now he'd had the chance to regain them.

But he must have known that regaining his wings had meant he would become *this*. He wouldn't just turn into some weird-looking creature that could simply soar through the atmosphere, escape Earth's gravity, and move out into the universe. He wouldn't become something that would hide in the shadows and fly where he couldn't be observed by humans.

No. He'd taken that feather knowing he would end up killing people. Hurting people he knew. Hunting them.

He'd hunted Castro. He'd known I would follow. It was me he really wanted.

That thought made me shiver even more violently. He wanted me. But what for? What use could one human be to him that the other humans had not been?

Fish's odd swooping asymmetrical wing beats changed and I felt us drop through the snow and clouds. We were headed toward the ground.

I had no idea what Fish wanted, but I was about to find out.

12

Fish let go of me and I dropped several feet into the snow.

Fucking snow. I hated the cold, but especially being cold and wet. Bad enough that January, February, and even March could be one long frozen gray tunnel with only the occasional hint of sunshine to give off a promise of spring, but when that tunnel was long, gray, frozen, *and* full of snow, sleet, or ice? That was so much worse.

Snow was pretty in pictures, not real life.

I caught my breath and looked around. The area was wooded and in the shadow of a cliff face to my right. At the base of the cliff was a bubbling creek that apparently had defied winter and hadn't frozen over completely.

Gray tree trunks stretched toward the sky, naked, their finger-like twigs looking like some kind of odd multi-armed monster begging the heavens to drop their blessings upon the woods. The forest floor was covered in snow, but some old tree trunks and reddish rocks stuck out from the fresh fall.

I saw nothing of Fish, though the swoosh of wings had not completely dissipated. He was still around somewhere. I couldn't worry about that, though. I had to think about survival. Hypothermia was already a danger; no doubt frostbite was as well. Had I been dropped here to freeze to death?

I spotted one dark red spot on the snow a few feet in front of me. Was I bleeding? Or was this from Fish?

I looked down at myself briefly but didn't see any blood on my clothes, just damp spots and flakes of snow.

I touched my sleeve, reassuring myself the blade was still there. I still had protection.

Not much protection, possibly, but at least some. I'd seen Fish get shot and be no worse for wear barely four days later. No matter how I cut him with this blade, he'd recover. Then what?

I pushed that thought aside. Before I could worry about hurting Fish later, I had to survive him now. The undergrowth here was minimal, so at least I could pick a direction to hike. Maybe walking would help warm me up; at the moment, all I could do was shiver. My knees were weak from the terror of the flight and exhaustion and cold. Walking for hundreds of yards, let alone miles, was the last thing I wanted to do. But no one was coming to rescue me, and staying on my feet and moving was probably my best chance for survival.

I put the creek and cliff to my back and began walking. My drenched jeans clung to my flesh, leaching even more warmth from my body. At this rate, even if I continued to have the strength to walk, I'd be frozen stiff inside an hour.

I wandered through the woods, aware that the sun was getting lower in the sky. Clouds of fog from my breath wreathed themselves around my head as I struggled to keep going.

Unfortunately, I had no idea where I was, and the trees all looked the same. After a while, I turned around, but the cliff was so far enough away that I couldn't see it. All around me, the woods looked the same. Only the direction of the shadows gave the world three dimensions; otherwise, the world around me was nothing but white snow, gray trees, and the occasional rock or stump. But distances were difficult to judge in the near monochromatic wilderness.

My heart was in turmoil. For all I knew, I could be walking in exactly the wrong direction. Perhaps I should have climbed the cliff somehow and looked at the woods from a higher perspective.

Too late now. I could try to follow my footsteps back to where Fish had dropped me, but by then it would probably be dark and I wouldn't see anything.

I kept walking, though I realized that the more I walked, the slower I was going. My feet had long since gone numb and now simply shot spikes of pain up my legs. My arms and body trembled violently and my teeth chattered together so much I was surprised they hadn't broken already.

As the sun sank below the horizon, my strength finally gave out. I knew nothing but pain and cold. Whoever had said freezing to death was a gentle, peaceful and painless death should rot in hell for telling such a lie.

Anger filled me. I lifted my face toward the overcast sky and tried to shout, but only a whisper escaped my frozen throat. "What do you want with me?"

I thought I heard a wing flap, and I whirled around, but the darkening wood was just trees and snow as far as I could see, which wasn't very far now.

The red-hot anger in my chest felt good. It made me feel more alive, more grounded in the world, and a touch less cold.

But my numb legs wouldn't hold me up. I leaned against a tree and slid to the ground. Wet snow seeped through my jeans again. I was almost too cold to shiver now.

My head felt heavy and my chin touched my chest. Was this how I was going to die? Ware thought I was so special, and I was going to freeze to death like a regular mortal, even if I could count my descent from his ancient dead-but-not-quite-dead lover.

I couldn't miss the absurdity of my plight.

The heat in my chest tumbled into my stomach; a sudden nausea gripped me. The nausea turned into a stabbing pain. I felt hungry in a way I never had before; nausea and hunger were not a good combination.

Is that what happened to you when you froze to death? You got hungry? Angry? Sported a red-hot stone in the center of your chest that burned you until the pain made it difficult to breathe?

Something thumped beside me. I opened my eyes to see red feathers that glimmered in the last dying rays of the sunset.

I sat at the base of the tree and waited for the end. I had no strength left, and a bizarre sudden rush of hunger wasn't useful in turning aside the wrath of the being in front of me.

Fish looked at me oddly, the shorter feathers around his face and surrounding his head rippling in something I perceived as confusion.

"You wanted me out here," I said, my voice almost too quiet for me to hear myself. Every part of me seemed frozen to near-immobility, as if my very cells were being replaced by ice. "You let me walk through the woods until I was too cold to fight you. Why hesitate now?"

He lunged at me, then stopped and hopped to the side, and I saw the disappointment in his midnight black eyes. He was playing with his food. He'd dropped me here, followed me through the forest, wanted to chase me down like a dog with a rabbit. He wanted the excitement of pursuit. He wanted a game.

Well, that hadn't gone as expected, had it? I was too cold and too weak to go another step, let alone run quickly enough to be chased down.

Fish crept forward and I watched, both horrified at the sight of my oncoming death, and fascinated by the alien way in which he moved. It wasn't just the wings or the shiny feathers. *Everything* about him screamed that he was not made by this world, and did not belong here.

Without warning, he sprang at me. The moment his razor-sharp talons touched me and drew blood, the orb of anger in my chest exploded.

Fire flared throughout my body. My right hand grabbed the knife that was still up the left sleeve of my coat. I drew it out and stabbed the creature in what, for a human, would be the gut.

Fish flung himself away from me with a shocked scream and landed on the forest floor.

I stood, the fire in my veins giving me strength. Steam rose from my wet clothing as my heated flesh dried out my clothes from the inside.

"Come at me again," I growled in a low voice I did not recognize.

Fish hesitated, one hand moving toward the new hole in his flesh I'd just made. But I kept my eyes on his and knew he wouldn't leave here without me. He'd built up this hunt too much in his mind. One thrust from this blade wouldn't be enough to put him off. The blood he was smelling was his own, but it was still blood. He would want to smell more.

I waved the blade in his direction and growled. Somewhere, in the back of my mind, I was alarmed by that, but mostly, I was defiant and angry. Fish had killed people; he'd maimed Castro; he'd kidnapped me and was now pursuing me for his own amusement. Nothing he'd done was excusable. He needed to be hurt.

I needed to be the one to hurt him.

Fish darted to the side, but kept his eyes on me, and I wasn't fooled by the feint. The moment he turned toward me, I leaped on him and stabbed him again, this time in the upper arm.

He brought his talons to bear and scraped them across my back, but I rolled away and stood up before he could truly shred my flesh. I still had multiple layers of clothing between my skin and his claws. It wasn't exactly armor, but it was something. Anything that helped me withstand his attacks for even a few seconds was good.

Fish circled me, keeping his eyes on me all the while. I realized he was holding his wings stiffly behind him, as if he didn't want me to even see them.

That was where he would be the most vulnerable. Despite the fact I'd stabbed him twice already, he wasn't bothering to protect his chest, his neck, his face, his abdomen. The body parts that he would want to protect as a human weren't what concerned him. He didn't even seem to mind that he was injured. I needed to target his wings.

It seemed unlikely he would let me get that close to them. I had to come up with a plan. Quickly.

13

The creature in front of me clacked its needle-like teeth together. I realized the teeth had previously struck me as looking as if they had been made from chrome, and now they might as well have been dull pewter. The sun had set and any remaining twilight would be gone quickly. The clouds had thinned and moonlight made them glow. That light wasn't much but at least I wasn't stuck in the woods fighting something that wanted to kill me while wrapped in complete darkness.

I couldn't stand here staring at Fish's alien form all night. The heat that seemed to be stretching and pulling every muscle from the inside couldn't last forever, right? This was simply some weird side-effect of being so cold. My body was confused and shutting down and somehow making me feel hot and nauseated when I was actually cold and slowly freezing to death.

I feinted to my left, then swiped at Fish with my right hand. He hopped out of range easily. I slipped to my knees; despite my newfound strength, I wasn't supernaturally strong like my opponent. I had to be quick about this.

I took a deep breath. Maybe something supremely stupid, exactly the sort of thing Fish might expect from a weak human like myself, was the way to go.

Desperate times and all that. I clenched the blade in my right hand more tightly, and turned my back on Fish as if I were planning to make a run for it. I even took a couple of steps before whirling around and slashing with the knife.

As I had hoped, he had gotten closer, but not close enough for me to injure. He'd seen through my ruse. Well, not terribly surprising, I guess.

My eyesight wavered and I felt something trickling down my back into my jeans. Damn. My back was bleeding. I hadn't thought he'd slashed all the way through my clothing but he had. At least I couldn't bleed to death from some shallow slashes on my back.

I guess.

Even if I couldn't bleed to death, I could still be weakened by blood loss. Time was not on my side. All Fish had to do was stand back and watch me weaken until he got bored and finished me off.

Fine. I had little choice but to be bold. I pretended to turn again, then spun back and rushed right at Fish, knife held out in front of me.

He'd darted forward, so I threw myself onto him. His sharp feathers bit into my face and my hands. I tried to reach around his shoulders and jab the knife into the joint where his wings met his shoulders, but he managed to grab my wrist and push my hand away.

His teeth came down on my left shoulder and I screamed. Numbness spread down my left arm; if I'd been holding the knife in that hand, I would have dropped it.

Suddenly, something thumped into Fish's side with an angry squawk.

Cookie. Somehow, the scrap had found me. Tears of both pain and gratitude sprang up in my eyes, getting caught on the frost on my eyelashes

Fish's grasp on my shoulder lessened. I pulled back as Cookie squawked again, this time being muffled as it had something covering its face.

I jerked backward as Fish's jaws let go. I saw Cookie holding onto the side of Fish's head, hands wrapped around his razor-sharp feathers.

Black blood oozed from Cookie's hands as well as Fish's head. Fish raised his hands to pull Cookie away.

While Fish was momentarily distracted, I darted forward and stabbed at the base of a wing.

Fish's scream filled the night air. It shook the trees, and sliced through every bone in my body, making me gasp at the volume of it. My knees gave out and I thumped butt-first onto the forest floor. The shocked traveled up my spine and rattled my skull.

Fish turned toward me and the handle of the knife was pulled out of my hands, leaving the blade buried in his flesh.

Cookie landed on the ground and stood between me and Fish. It stood on all fours like a football player waiting for the ball to be snapped. Its hide looked darker than usual; I could not tell if that were because of the darkness or its own black blood covering it.

Fish twisted around, trying to grab the handle of the blade, but he couldn't reach the base of his wings with his hands.

Cookie had obviously taken in the situation. It flung itself onto Fish's shoulder and grabbed the handle of the knife. I expected Cookie would try to pull it out to return it to me, but before I could warn it not to do that, it pushed the blade even farther into Fish's flesh.

Fish screamed again. I ran forward and also grabbed the handle. It was now buried in Fish's body all the way to the hilt. Cookie kept trying to push it farther in.

"Stop," I said in the low growly voice that seemed to have settled into my throat.

Cookie froze, then hopped off Fish. I yanked the blade out of Fish's body and shoved it into the base of his wing. Fish pushed himself off the ground and extended his wings.

He was going to try to fly away.

"No, you don't," I said. "You stay right here." I pulled out the knife and stabbed him in the base of the other wing.

Fish lay sprawled on the snow, which was now marred by the thrashing of his body and the footsteps of the three of us. The moon broke out of the cloud cover for a moment, revealing bright red, dark red, and black blood mixed together in splashes and puddles everywhere.

Fish's screams had become desperate. The heat inside my body grew as if responding to his despair, as if my well-being were served by his pain.

I took the blade in my bloody hand. Touching it caused a bright purple spark which shocked me and made my teeth rattle, but which didn't keep me from holding onto the handle and taking possession of the blade once again.

The tattoo of Ware's name on my palm was on fire, and that fire joined the heat in my veins. As if the heat were a light, my vision cleared as if the dark night around me had suddenly become twilight once again. The line of Fish's wing where it joined his shoulder was obvious to me, and the rippling of the muscles underneath the feathers was now visible.

I sliced into one wing, and cut the tendons—if, indeed, tendon was even the right word here—keeping his wings attached to his body. Fish rolled away and, once again, I lost my grip on the handle.

Cookie took up the fight, jumping onto Fish and twisting the blade. A fresh gout of dark blood poured out of Fish's shoulder. I got my knees under me and crawled back to Fish, who was now flopping around on the ground like a, well, fish on the river bank.

I pinned Fish's left arm under my knee while Cookie continued to twist the knife. Fish howled but Cookie didn't relent.

"Thanks," I said. "I'll take it from here." My voice still held a raspy quality I did not recognize, but I didn't care. I simply needed to get this done.

I reached for the knife and was stopped by the color of the blood on my hands. It was...blue? Surely that wasn't right. And I could swear it was glowing.

I almost giggled. It was too funny. Glowing blue blood? I was clearly hallucinating from the cold. The heat that continued to surge through my veins was a different kind of hallucination, if that were the right word. Anyway, the whole situation was absurd and completely unreal.

My hand smoked where the blue glowing blood lay on the palm. The brand of Ware's name now glowed even more brilliantly than the blood, but in red rather than blue.

A dark smear across my hands must have been Cookie's blood. The blue substance seemed to be a combination of my blood, Fish's blood, and the scrap's blood. All come together on my palm, lighting up Ware's name glyph.

Fish twisted his upper body as much as he could, his gaze captivated by the glowing brand. I held it out to him. "See that? What do you think of that?"

Fish closed his eyes and turned away. He moved slightly and I realized he was trying to get his hands underneath him. If he managed that, he could push himself off the ground, knock me off.

I couldn't let that happen. Too much blood had been shed today to let this creature get away with so much murder. I yanked the blade out of Fish's wing joint and began slicing through his flesh.

He screamed but I didn't hesitate. With a few more quick slices, the right wing was free from the shoulder.

Fish's screams went from pain to something else entirely. Despair, maybe.

Cookie grabbed the wing and dragged it away, but even as the scrap worked to get the thing away from Fish, it began smoking. Within a few moments, it had caught fire and seconds later, it had become ash.

Cookie jumped backward, then sniffed the small pile of ash warily, making a confused chirp.

Triumphantly, I grabbed the remaining wing. Fish wriggled feebly beneath me, but his strength was ebbing.

Someone grabbed me by the shoulders and pulled me off of my foe. Air whistled by my ears as I was thrown across the woods. Luckily, I didn't smack right into a tree.

Or else whoever had pulled me off hadn't wanted me to and was good at tossing people with precision.

I landed on the cold ground and dropped the knife once more. As I struggled to get my hands and feet under me, I heard the crunch of footsteps in the snow. The footsteps stopped nearby. I blinked. Someone tall was bending over me. The person stood up quickly and the blade glinted in their hand.

I was going to die now. Whoever had come here to rescue Fish was also here to kill me. I should have been terrified, but it was difficult to feel anything around this raging inferno in my veins. It still pushed its way into every fiber and gave me strength. However, I knew I had to be exhausted and near-frozen. I would die here by cold or by a magic ancient knife.

The person standing over me didn't stab me, though. Maybe I could still escape this if I stayed on the ground and the person thought I was too injured or exhausted or cold to get up. A light ray of hope tucked itself around my heart, beating back the fires just a tiny, tiny bit.

Where was Cookie? Wouldn't it help me now? I tried yelling out for it, but my throat would only make a guttural angry sound.

"Don't be angry with me," said a deep voice.

Pellagrio. He was another Forlorn, one I didn't care for.

"I can see why Ware was worried about you," he said. "Imagine doing what you just did. Slicing off the wing of a Forlorn, and you just some little Lost human."

I tried saying *not just some little Lost human* but my voice still refused to cooperate; the growl I made was even lower and angrier than before.

"Come on, then," said Pellagrio, his voice now farther away than it was. He no longer seemed to be speaking to me.

I sat up. What had been a metallic and crystal creature out of someone's deepest nightmare had changed. It was now half creature, half human, but the halves wavered and changed, so that at one moment, Fish's left hand was covered in razor-sharp metal-looking feathers, and in the next, those feathers had been absorbed into his skin somehow, but he had sprouted feathers further up his arm. Then the feathers slid out of the skin of his chest before disappearing and feathers then wrapped around his neck. My eyes refused to track the constant shifting and transforming of Fish's flesh, as if my brain couldn't take in the weirdness. His face wavered in an in between state; one eye large and deepest black, the other human and weeping.

"No no no," cried Fish before the feathers covered the lower part of his face and the sounds he made changed from English to something else entirely.

Pellagrio lifted the shrieking Fish and tossed him over a shoulder. Fish's screams turned into moans.

Pellagrio came back to me and offered me the hand that wasn't holding on to Fish.

"You need to get cleaned up," said Pellagrio. "I didn't realize, when Ware asked me to track your little scrap friend, that you wouldn't need my help. At least, not against Fish. For the rest of it, you'll need Ware."

None of that made sense. Did I care? Should I care? The world wavered and I didn't know what to think. Or feel. Or even what I *could* think or feel around this new thing, this conflagration, in my body.

It was eating away at me, like any fire. But I didn't feel as if I were turning in to ash. Whatever was happening to me, it was doing something to me that I didn't understand.

Pellagrio seemed to think Ware would know what to say and do to fix me. To make me myself again.

Cookie jumped up onto my shoulder and I wearily trudged behind Pellagrio. I had no idea how far we had to walk, but it didn't matter. If I collapsed, Pellagrio would just have to get me to his vehicle somehow. That was no longer my concern.

My thoughts faded away until nothing existed but the dark snow-filled world around me, Fish's whimpers, and the remaining heat in my body. A heat I didn't understand and that would consume me.

I was too exhausted for that to frighten me right now. I just knew that I was being consumed and something else was taking my place.

What that was, I had no idea.

14

I had no real way to know how far we walked until we got to Pellagrio's car, an ancient sedan with peeling olive-green paint and worn beige interior.

Pellagrio threw a now-silent Fish into the trunk of the car and slammed it shut. I simply stood, exhausted, and wondering how long it would take for the fire in my body to actually turn into actual flames and burn me to death.

Pellagrio opened the passenger side front door. Cookie chirped in my ear, hopped down from my shoulder, and climbed into the car.

"Well?" Pellagrio asked. "Get in. You waiting for an invitation from the queen?"

He waited without moving. His entire being seemed rooted in the earth, as if he were solid like a boulder. Something unmovable. But that wasn't why I disliked him; he was also an ass. My first meeting with him, he'd called me a *bitch* and tried to intimidate me. Ware had burst out of his office and had thrown Pellagrio out of the bar.

I slid into the seat and sat there. Pellagrio came around the car and got in. The car had been parked on the shoulder of a rural road. I didn't recognize the place. Pellagrio had to do a five-point turn to get the huge sedan turned around and headed back the way he had apparently come.

I simply stared out the front window. After several miles and a few turns, I saw a sign for I-55. Pellagrio maneuvered the car onto the highway, which was only lightly dusted with snow at this point. The snow plows had been busy and efficient.

The world passed by while I was eerily calm and quiet. Only the molten metal in my veins held my attention. What was it?

By the time we approached downtown, my brain had started to work again. I saw the building of Barnes-Jewish Hospital in the distance and memories of this afternoon came flooding back.

Castro. Fish had nearly killed him. How could I have forgotten him for even a moment?

I sat up in the car seat and suddenly realized I wasn't wearing a seatbelt. I also realized I was dripping with sweat. The heat in my body had been making my body try to force my temperature down. I didn't think it had worked, or at least not yet. I felt as if I were in a sauna, despite the snow outside the car.

"Castro," I managed to croak. Whatever had controlled my voice had at least loosened its grasp for a moment.

"If he were dead, we wouldn't be headed for the hospital, would we?" asked Pellagrio. "Ware said to drop you off there." He glanced over at me. "But first, you'll need to change. You're covered in blood and a serious amount of gore. I picked up some stuff from your apartment; it's in the back seat with your scrap."

Indignation that Pellagrio had simply broken into my apartment, and could speak about it so unapologetically, made me move my head for the first time since I got in the car. I looked at him with disdain.

"Really?" I whispered. "My apartment?"

Pellagrio didn't respond. I didn't really expect him to. The high-handedness of the Forlorn when it came to my personal life hadn't started with him, and no doubt, wouldn't end here, either. Boundaries were something these people needed to learn about.

Pellagrio turned the car into a parking garage, and drove to an elevator. "Here," he said. "Get the clothes, change, then go in the building, follow the signs to the ICU. Make sure to take the scrap with you; I'm not interested in watching it for you."

I refrained from saying Cookie didn't need watching, partly because I had no idea what "watching it" might mean, and partly because I didn't want to open my mouth and discover the growl had overtaken my voice again. I was beginning to be freaked out that something, or someone, had more control of my voice than I did.

As I quickly ditched my soiled clothing for fresh, I had an even more terrifying thought: what if nothing had control over my voice except me? What would that mean? Who was I? What was I? What would I become if I kept hanging around supernatural creatures who wanted me as a pawn in their wars?

Once I'd finished dressing, I headed for the elevator.

"I'm not staying," said Pellagrio as he got back into the car. "I've got to do something with what's in the trunk. You find your own way home from here."

I pressed the button for the elevator and didn't respond. Castro was here somewhere. Everything else could wait.

I turned to Cookie. "You stay here. I'll be back in a while."

Cookie wavered, clearly wanting to be with me. But after a few moments, it crawled under a nearby car and sat with arms crossed in front of it. It looked annoyed, but I knew it would stay.

The elevator arrived and I got in, eager to get to Castro. I pushed the button for the ICU level and paced impatiently while it lifted me to the correct floor.

The elevator let me out into the hospital building and I followed the signs until I got to the ICU. Ware stood in the corridor. I assume he could keep humans from questioning him if necessary; it wasn't as if he were invisible, either, but people didn't seem to notice him if he didn't want them to. Since it was far past any reasonable visitor's hours, he had to have either argued with someone successfully that he should stay, or no one was questioning his right to be here in the middle of the night.

I would bet on the latter.

He walked toward me quickly. "He's here, he's alive," he said as he put one hand under my right elbow as if to help me keep my feet.

He guided me toward a bed where I saw a white-sheeted figure hooked up to various machines. The machines beeped in a comforting way; as if their quiet insistence on recording Castro's life signs were joyful news they needed to announce to the world.

I ignored Ware and stood by the bed. Dimly, I realized that Ware had retreated, but I had very little attention for anything beyond the scene of Castro in the bed.

He looked small and frail, almost bloodless pale. He was only a little taller than me so to see him looking so small in the wide hospital bed was a shock.

The heat inside my body surged again, purging the tears that had threatened to come. Instead, I grabbed Castro's hand and closed my eyes. He had to recover; he had to come home. What would Petunia and I do without him?

Visions of Castro in our apartment filled my mind. Castro making pancakes for a movie-watching night. Castro quietly talking to Petunia as he gave her fresh water. Castro smiling at me in the morning when I woke up as grumpy as usual, which he found funny for some reason. Castro worrying endlessly over his hair in the mirror.

He was funny, supportive, kind, generous, and even a bit of an oddball. Although it was me who'd gotten wrapped up in the supernatural, it was Castro who'd been interested in cryptids and the paranormal for his whole life. He had notebooks full of articles on hauntings, Bigfoot sightings, poltergeists, time slips, interdimensional portals, skinwalkers, UFOs, the skunk ape, and anything else that caught his interest. If it were weird and unexplainable, Castro wanted to read about it.

Hell, he probably wanted to experience it. He'd once mentioned he'd love to go to the Mothman Festival someday; we'd never been able to afford to do something like that, but it was on our to-do list for the future.

Castro's bucket list included wandering the Winchester House; staying at the Stanley Hotel; going on a ghost tour of the Eastern State Penitentiary in Pennsylvania; hiking through the Pine Barrens of New Jersey; and visiting the St. Augustine Lighthouse, among other things. I silently swore to him that if we survived until summer, we would do all those things, and more. We would indulge Castro's interest and explore his hobbies to his heart's content, whatever Ware and his supernatural buddies thought.

After all, it was their fault Castro was here in the hospital. Some of the Forlorn had wanted to hurt him because of his proximity to me and Ware. I'd had no idea how to keep him safe, but it was impossible in any case. Because of his hobbies, Castro hadn't been nearly as cautious of the Forlorn as he should have been. He had been especially drawn to Fish, who was normally so pitiful and broken, as if kindness toward Fish could not only assuage Castro's curiosity, but help heal that creature's soul.

Fish had repaid that kindness with cruelty and pain.

The heat in my soul flared up again, but this time without the nausea. In fact, my stomach seemed to be settling down. I took a deep breath; it scorched my throat and I winced. But the second breath was less bad. By the fourth breath, breathing was no longer painful. Even the raging inferno inside my body, though not gone, had become tame. Controllable. I felt more like myself than I had since Fish had dropped me off in the wilderness.

"Teryl, what are you doing?"

Ware grabbed me around the waist and lifted me off the ground. He dragged me backward.

I opened my eyes and glanced around furiously. "What? What's going on? Let me go!"

"Teryl, you can't do this," said Ware.

The alarm in his voice startled me and I stopped struggling. I was aware then of scrub-attired people rushing past us and the wretched beeping of alarms.

"What's...what's going on?" I asked.

Ware pulled us back against the wall as more people came in pushing something laden with instruments and unidentifiable medical things.

"Castro?" I asked, my heart sinking.

I listened to what the hospital personnel were shouting to each other but I couldn't comprehend what was happening. The alarms kept up their wailing while I watched, heart pounding far more quickly than I could remember it ever had before.

The yelling faded into the background as I noticed the monitor had several colored lines on it. The lines weren't quite flat, but almost. The small variations did not seem to have rhyme or reason to them. I might not know what they meant, but it was clear they indicated something very, very bad.

Fear flooded me and the heat in my veins, at long last, sputtered and went out. "What did Fish do? What did he do?"

"He didn't," said Ware. "Be still. Don't distract them. I can keep them from noticing us, at least for a while, but not if you keep struggling and yelling."

I went limp, exhausted by the flames that had gutted my interior for hours, and now by the terror of what was happening with Castro. The bustling people around his bedside seemed to know what they were doing; they moved competently, confidently, and quickly.

I did my best to be as still as Ware had instructed, but I desperately wanted to get to Castro. My whole being was focused on him. So many people stood around the bed, that nothing was visible to me except one foot.

The foot was extraordinarily pale. It moved crazily as the people around the bed did things I didn't understand to the man in the bed.

I became dizzy; it wasn't until my body automatically sucked in a huge lungful of air that I realized I'd been holding my breath.

The activity around the bed lasted for several minutes. The dizziness continued as every fiber of muscle in my body began trembling with desperation and complete exhaustion.

"He has to be okay," I said. "He has to."

Slowly, the activity ceased. The people around the bed stepped back. "Call it," said one.

"What?" I whispered. Even I knew that meant they were recording the time of death. *Death*.

Castro couldn't be dead. He couldn't.

No!

Someone was screaming incoherently. I stared at the figure on the bed and threw myself at it. But Ware's grip was too tight. He pulled me backward.

The screaming continued and I finally realized it was me. The figures around Castro's bed now realized I was there. They turned, almost as one, and someone shouted, "What are you doing here? Get out!"

I kept struggling but Ware merely held me even more tightly and marched down the hall. He bypassed the elevator and flung us into the stairwell. I continued struggling but he jogged down the stairs as if carrying a writhing screaming human was no burden at all.

Ware flung open a second door and cold air blasted me as Ware strode into the parking garage. Finally, he released me. I immediately sprung back toward the door to the stairs, but Ware caught me a second time.

"No, Teryl," he said. "He's gone."

"He can't be," I gasped. "He can't. Fish..."

"It wasn't Fish," said Ware softly as he clasped me to his chest. "It was you."

15

My brain refused to understand what Ware said.

"What?" My voice broke when I said it.

Ware wrapped his arms around me in a gesture I took to be more hug than restraint. "It was you, Teryl. I had hoped I was wrong and that I was misreading the signs. But it seems you're undergoing a kind of transformation that Zireya foretold. It started that first night, when I drew my name on your hand. Everything that's happened since then has only served to accelerate this process. At least, I think so. It's not like this has happened before to one of the Lost."

The brand on my right palm. "So, this is your fault?" I managed to ask in between great gulps of air. My throat was raw from my screams. My flesh felt like it might fall off my bones; as if I could literally fall apart. The world had no color; even sound was dulled and my ears seemed to want to refuse to hear as they should. Everything was if I were underwater.

"No, not like you mean," he said. "I'm at fault for not being more forthcoming. But it was Yama who did this to you."

Yama? I hadn't seen that Forlorn for months. He generally looked like a portly Asian man, but through Oya's eyes, I had seen his coppery and gold winged form for a moment. He What could he have had to do with this?

"Remember last summer," said Ware. His voice sounded as if he were dragging the words out in the same way he'd dragged me out of the hospital. "Yama did something to you so you could control what Oya was doing to you. For lack of a better word, Yama is a master of poison. A form of poison flows in his veins; that's what he shared with you."

My mind latched onto that word. "He poisoned me?"

"In a way. He had no way of knowing how it would affect you. If he'd done it to another of the Lost, it would have slowly poisoned them, possibly to death, but perhaps only to the point of crippling their health. But it did more to you than anyone would have believed."

"So this is Yama's fault?"

"Yes, and no," he said. "We all know the prophecy, but no one knew for certain who it was talking about. I suspected it might be you, and so did Yama, and Oya, and a few others. But we had no proof. I think something happened today that triggered a change that should have come more slowly. I didn't understand what happened to you today or I'd never have let you near Castro."

"Save him," I whispered.

"I can't." His voice was so wretched I believed him. And that was when the tears came.

Ware continued to hold me, and I cried until I had nothing left inside me. And then I cried more. At some point, I realized Cookie had wrapped itself around my right leg and was making cooing sounds. I could find no comfort I that right now.

Eventually, I had nothing left inside me. No grief, no tears, no caring. I was empty.

Ware picked me up like a baby and carried me to a car. He laid me in the passenger seat. Cookie jumped in the car and sat in my lap, staring my in the face. I wouldn't make eye contact with it. I paid no attention to the world.

At some point, the car stopped. I couldn't even lift my head. What did it matter if I ever moved again? Castro was dead.

I'd killed him. Fish may have injured him, but I was the one who had killed him in the end. My own heart felt as if it should stop beating in shame and guilt.

I went limp as Ware carried me into the back of the building that housed the Angels' Share.

Ware didn't go all the way into the main room, though. He turned aside and took me into his private office.

He laid me on the leather couch I'd sat on once before, the single previous time I'd been in this room. He covered me with a blanket.

Cookie jumped up on the couch and snuggled up in between my ribcage and arm. I closed my eyes and turned my face away from the room.

Ware took my hand. "I can't make it better," he said. "But I will be here to do what I can."

I didn't care. He held my hand and I just closed my eyes and wished to die.

A week later, I stood at the side of a freshly-filled grave and dashed away more tears.

The service had been very simple. Neither Castro nor I had much use for religion, and now that I knew that stories of demons and angels and gods were based on creatures like my boss, I had no desire to even think about religion ever again.

Castro had a few friends, including Andre and his cousin Brooklyn, who had come. Ware was standing off to the side, but I had specifically requested no other Forlorn should show. I wasn't speaking to any of them and hoped not to see another fucking alien for the rest of my life.

I knew that wasn't going to happen, but pretending it was possible was the only thing holding me together these days.

The only other attendant was Cookie. The scrap had spent the week doing its best to be useful, insofar as it understood being useful. Brooklyn had even trained it to put dishes away and to scrub the floors. Now it stood to the side, whimpering a low, sad tune.

"I'll drive you home," said Brooklyn. Her hair, which I'd seen in various shades of red and purple, was now electric blue. The shade suited her.

I nodded and headed toward her car. She had been staying over and taking care of Petunia since Ware had brought me back to the apartment the day after Castro had died.

The day after I'd killed him.

The knowledge I'd killed Castro still ate at me. It was like a cancer in my chest that kept trying to smash its way out of my ribs, to make my guilt obvious to everyone.

Every moment I was near Brooklyn, I felt desperate to tell her the truth. And equally desperate to keep it unspoken, as if *not* saying anything could make this all be some horrible nightmare. If I didn't speak of it, then maybe Castro wasn't really dead.

It didn't matter that I knew he was dead. Somehow, my heart wanted to deny it, and keeping quiet about what had killed him seemed to be the only way to do that.

Brooklyn was clearly worried about me, but I didn't care. Every day, I thought about how easy it might be to jump off the apartment building roof. Or to just stop eating. Or to wander into traffic.

When Brooklyn hadn't been nearby, someone else was. I wasn't sure who, though I was nearly positive it wasn't Ware. Pellagrio, maybe. He might not like me, but he acknowledged Ware's authority, or perhaps, dominance, over him. If Ware told him to watch me, he would.

Not Oya. She and Mia were still waiting for the arrival of their child. Every weather expert in the country had found a way to get to St. Louis this week to record the odd lightning storms that continued over Lafayette Square and refused to move off with the rest of the weather patterns.

I didn't care about that, either. Nothing moved me, except knowing that Petunia was well cared-for. She had been Castro's baby; more than anything else in the apartment, she was a reminder of him, and I couldn't care for her the way I should. Brooklyn was adopting her, which seemed to be the perfect solution.

I'd spent a lot of the week before the funeral throwing out Castro's stuff, and some of my stuff as well. Brooklyn had watched me do it, and helped if I asked, but otherwise, appeared to assume this was something I had to do myself.

She was right about that.

The apartment was nearly empty now, as empty as I had become. It was the shell of a home as much as I was now a shell of a person. I couldn't stay there. It would cost to get out of the lease, but I bet Ware would be good for it.

Before we got to Brooklyn's car, we were stopped by Ware, who stood between us and our goal.

"I need to speak to her," he said to Brooklyn. "It will only take a minute."

Brooklyn gave me a look; I had the feeling she would have tried to fight off Ware if I'd asked. But I just shrugged. I didn't care what he had to say. I didn't care if he spoke, walked away, or suddenly started singing Broadway show tunes.

Brooklyn walked away, calling for Cookie to follow her. To my surprise, it did just that. She had it better trained than I thought.

"Teryl," Ware said after Brooklyn was out of earshot. "I'm sorry about Castro. I'm sorry I didn't realize soon enough what was going on. Now you need to know more. Also, if you want to control, or even stop, what's happening to you, you need to go to her."

I merely stood staring out at the cemetery gates. Brooklyn had reached her car and had started it. She opened the passenger side door, I assume so we could have a quick getaway if necessary.

"Come to the Angels' Share," he said. "I'll give you instructions on how to reach her."

I kept staring.

"You need to understand what's happening," said Ware. "And, as it hasn't happened before, I don't have a lot of information to share. But she will."

"She," I said flatly.

"Zireya."

I shook my head. Zireya was dead, or at least as near to dead as the Forlorn could get. I couldn't speak with her.

"She can help," he said. "Otherwise, this power is going to destroy you, and everyone around you. Castro will only be the first you kill."

"I won't kill anyone else," I said.

"But you will," he said. His voice was low and emotionless and, somehow, was all the more believable for that. "Please. Learn to control this power, or how to put it down. I can't guide you in this. Only you and she together can figure this out."

I hesitated, but why not? If anything, perhaps I could find a way to die and follow Castro into oblivion. Or perhaps I would turn into a scrap like Cookie and be a small, nearly mindless creature with no memory of my former life.

Either way, I wouldn't exist anymore. Teryl Gray would be well and truly gone, just like Castro.

I bit back a sob at the thought of Castro; the way his wet black hair stuck out at all angles from his head when he got out of the shower, or the way he laughed at funny movies. The anger he felt every time he read about another case of child abuse.

"Fine," I said. "When and where?"

"Go home, get the flute you got in London, come to the bar," he said. "Tonight. Between you and Cookie and Pellagrio, the trip will be as safe as I can make it. Not safe, but you'll do better with companions than you would alone."

What did I care if I were alone? If I died?

"Whatever. I'll be there."

"Good," he said. He reached out awkwardly with one hand and patted me on the shoulder. The gesture was hesitant and said more about his disturbed state of mind than anything else could have. Ware was always so sure of himself, always so composed.

But not now.

I walked to Brooklyn's car and got inside.

"What did he want?" she asked.

"Nothing," I said. "Not a goddam thing."

Cookie curled up on my lap. I petted it absently while Brooklyn took me home.

At least tonight, I would do something dangerous. Something that would kill me, or perhaps offer me a chance at atonement.

Like I could ever atone for what I'd done.

Cookie purred and sighed, happy to be near me. Didn't it understand that being near me meant it could be destroyed?

Thunder rumbled over the city. Ware had more to worry about than the errand he was sending me on. But the rest of it had nothing to do with me.

I had a job to do. What it entailed or how it would end was immaterial. In fact, if it meant I could face my ancestress and scream at her for what she'd done to me through her efforts to breed a Forlorn-human hybrid, then I was eager to go. I'd end the bitch if at all possible. For Castro's sake.

A strand of anger threaded its way around my ribs. Not the horrific burning of Yama's poison or the hunger of Zireya's power, just ordinary human anger. I'd take that and fling it in the goddam bitch's face before I clawed her eyes out.

That thought made me feel a little better.

I leaned back in the seat of the car and continued to pet Cookie. Brooklyn looked over.

"You look better than you have since...since it happened," she said.

"Yeah," I said. "I'm sure I do."

About the Author

 Marella Sands is a native St. Louisan who has published novels, novellas, short stories, a poem, an essay, and non-fiction works. Her historical novels, *Sky Knife* and *Serpent and Storm*, were set in 5th century Central America. In addition, she co-wrote two King's Quest novels with fellow St. Louisan Mark Sumner under the name Kenyon Morr. She has had short stories in several anthologies. She has always been interested in cemeteries, sits on the board of one, and also is a volunteer at Cahokia Mounds State Historic Site in Collinsville, Illinois (horseradish capital of the world and home of the world's largest ketchup bottle!). She and her husband travel whenever they can and stop by old cemeteries when they have the opportunity.

Marella earned degrees in anthropology from the University of Tulsa and Kent State University. The author's household includes the author, her husband, and a multitude of pets.

Contact Me!

Calling for anyone who wants to get their paranormal stories out! I'm currently researching a series which will feature UFOs, Bigfoot, shadow people, angels, demons, Ouija boards, and ghosts, among other things. I need personal stories to integrate into the series. If you're interested in sharing, contact me at **msands@marellasands.com**. You can be anonymous, or be identified by first name only, if that makes you more comfortable.

In the meantime, remember to check out my videos on YouTube. If you'd like to appear on my channel to push your book, your hobby, your small business, or your love of *The Lord of the Rings*, contact me.